Kept in the Dark

G·K
Hall
&Co.

*Also by Anthony Trollope
in Large Print:*

An Eye for an Eye

Kept in the Dark

Anthony Trollope

G.K. Hall & Co. • Thorndike, Maine

Originally published in 1882 and is now in Public Domain in the United States

G.K. Hall Large Print Perennial Bestseller Series.

The text of this Large Print edition is unabridged.
Other aspects of the book may vary from the original edition.

Set in 16 pt. Plantin by Al Chase.

Printed in the United States on permanent paper.

Library of Congress Cataloging-in-Publication Data

Trollope, Anthony, 1815–1882.
    Kept in the dark / Anthony Trollope.
      p.   cm.
    ISBN 0-7838-8767-1 (lg. print : hc : alk. paper)
    1. England — Social life and customs — 19th century — Fiction.
2. Married people — England — Fiction.   3. Large type books.
I. Title.
PR5684.K44 1999
823'.8 21—dc21
                                                     99-042032

Contents

Chapter I

CECILIA HOLT AND HER THREE FRIENDS

There came an episode in the life of Cecilia Holt which it is essential should first be told. When she was twenty-two years old she was living with her mother at Exeter. Mrs Holt was a widow with comfortable means, — ample that is for herself and her daughter to supply them with all required by provincial comfort and provincial fashion. They had a house without the city, with a garden and a gardener and two boys, and they kept a brougham, which was the joint care of the gardener and the boy inside and the boy outside. They saw their friends and were seen by them. Once in the year they left home for a couple of months and went — wherever the daughter wished. Sometimes there was a week or two in London; sometimes in Paris or Switzerland. The mother seemed to be only there to obey the daughter's behests, and Cecilia was the most affectionate of masters. Nothing could have been less disturbed or more happy than their lives. No doubt there was present in Cecilia's manner a certain looking down upon her mother, — of which all the world was aware, unless it was her mother and herself. The mother was not blessed by literary tastes, whereas Cecilia was great among French and German poets. And Cecilia was aesthetic, whereas the mother thought more of the delicate providing of the table. Cecilia had two or three female friends, who were not quite her equals in literature but nearly so. There was Maude Hippesley, the Dean's daughter, and Miss Altifiorla, the daughter of an Italian father, who had settled in Exeter with her maternal aunt, — in poor circumstances, but with an exalted opinion as to her own blood. Francesca Altifiorla was older than her friend, and was, perhaps, the least loved of the three, but the most often seen. And there was Mrs Green, the Minor Canon's wife, who had the advantage of a husband, but was nevertheless humble and retiring. They formed the *élite* of Miss Holt's society and were called by their Christian names. The Italian's name was Francesca and the married lady was called Bessy.

Cecilia had no lovers till there came in an evil hour into Exeter one Sir Francis Geraldine. She had somewhat scoffed at love, or at the necessity of having a lover. She and Miss Altifiorla had been of one mind on that subject. Maude Hippesley had a lover and could not be supposed to give her accord. Mrs Green had had one, but expressed an opinion that it was a trouble well over. A husband might be a comfort, but a lover was 'a bother'. 'It's such a blessing to be able to wear my old gloves before him. He doesn't mind it now as he knows he'll have to pay for the new.' But at length there came the lover. Sir Francis Geraldine was a man who had property in the county but had not lately lived upon it. He was of an old family of which he was very proud. He was an old baronet, a circumstance which he seemed to think was very much in his favour. Good heavens! From what a height did he affect to look down upon the peers of the last twenty years. His property was small, but so singular were his gifts that he was able to be proud of that also. It had all been in the possession of his family since the time of James I. And he was a man who knew everything though only forty, and by no means old in appearance. But if you were to believe him he had all that experience of the world which nothing but unlimited years could have given him. He knew all the Courts in Europe, and all the race courses, — and more especially all the Jacks and Toms who had grown into notoriety in those different worlds of fashion. He came to Exeter to stay with his brother-in-law, the Dean, and to look after his property for a while. There he fell in love with Cecilia Holt, and, after a fortnight of prosperous love-making, made her an offer. This the young lady accepted, averse as she was to lovers, and for a month was the happiest and proudest girl in all Exeter. The happiness and pride of a girl in her lover is something wonderful to behold. He is surely the only man, and she the only woman born worthy of such a man. She is to be the depository of all his secrets, and the recipient of all his thoughts. That other young ladies should accept her with submission in this period of her ecstasy would be surprising were it not that she is so truly exalted by her condition as to make her for a short period an object to them of genuine worship. In this way, for a month or six weeks, did Miss Holt's friends submit to her and bear with her. They endured to be considered but as the outside personages of an indifferent outer world, whereas Cecilia herself with her lover were the only two inhabitants of the small celestial empire in which they lived. Then there gradually came to be a change. And it must be acknowledged here that the change commenced with Cecilia Holt herself.

The greater the adoration of the girl the deeper the abyss into which she falls, — if she be doomed to fall at all. A month of imperfection she can bear, even though the imperfections be very glaring. For a month, or perhaps for six weeks, the desire to subject herself to a newly-found superior being supports her spirit against all trials. Neglect when it first comes is not known to be neglect. The first bursts of ill-temper have about them something of the picturesque, — or at any rate of the grotesque. Even the selfishness is displayed on behalf of an object so exalted as to be excusable. So it was with Cecilia Holt. The period of absolute, unmistaken, unreasonable love lasted but for six weeks after her engagement. During those six weeks all Exeter knew of it. There was no reticence on the part of anyone. Sir Francis Geraldine had fallen in love with Cecilia Holt and a great triumph had been won. Cecilia, in spite of her general well-

10

known objection to lovers, had triumphed a little. It is not to be supposed that she had miscarried herself outrageously. He is cold-hearted, almost cruel, who does not like to see the little triumph of a girl in such circumstances, who will not sympathise with her, and join with her, if occasion come, in her exaltation. No fault was found with Cecilia among her friends in Exeter, but it was a fact that she did triumph. How it was that the time of her worship then came to an end it would be difficult to say. She was perhaps struck by neglect, or something which appeared to her to be almost scorn. And the man himself, she found, was ignorant. The ill-temper had lost its picturesqueness, and became worse than grotesque. And the selfishness seemed to be displayed on an object not so high as to render it justifiable. Then came a fortnight of vacillating misery, in which she did not dare to tell her discomfort to either of her friends. Her mother, who though she could not read Schiller, was as anxious for her daughter's happiness as any mother could be, saw something of this and at last ventured to ask a question. 'Was not Francis to have been here this morning?'

Cecilia was at that moment thinking of her lover, thinking that he had been untrue to his tryst now for the third time; and thinking also that she knew him to be untrue not with any valid excuse, not with the slightest cause for an excuse, but with a pre-determination to show the girl to whom he was engaged that it did not

11

suit him any longer to be at the trouble of serving her. 'Oh, mamma, how foolish you are! How can I tell what Sir Francis Geraldine may be doing?'

'But I thought he was to have been here.'

'Mamma, please understand that I do not carry him about tied to my apron-strings. When it pleases him to come he will come.' Then she went on with her book and was silent for a minute or two. Then she broke out again. 'I am sure there ought to be a rule in life that people when they are engaged should never see each other again till they meet in the church.'

'I don't think that would do at all, my dear.'

'Perhaps things were different when you were young. The world becomes less simple every day. However, mamma, we must put up with Sir Francis whether he come or whether he remain away.'

'The world may be less simple,' said Mrs Holt after a pause, 'but I don't think it half so nice. Young men used to think that there was nothing so pleasant as a young lady's company when, — when, — when they were engaged, you know.' Then the conversation ended, and the morning passed without the coming of Sir Francis.

After that a week passed, — with great forbearance on the part of Cecilia. She thought herself at least to be forbearing. She thought much of her lover, and had no doubt tried to interest herself in the usual conversation of her friends. But they by the end of the week perceived that Sir Francis was never first spoken of by herself.

To Maude Hippesley it was very difficult to avoid an expression of her doubts, because Maude was niece to Sir Francis. And Sir Francis was much talked about at the Deanery. 'My uncle was not down here this morning,' Maude would say; — and then she would go on to excuse the defalcation. He had had business requiring his immediate attention, — probably something as to the marriage settlements. 'But of course he will tell you all that.' Cecilia saw through the little attempts. Maude was quite aware that Sir Francis was becoming weary of his lover cares, and made the best excuse she could for them. But Maude Hippesley never had liked her uncle.

'Oh, my dear Maude,' said Cecilia, 'pray let him do what he pleases with himself in these the last days of his liberty. When he has got a wife he must attend to her, — more or less. Now he is as free as air. Pray let him do as he pleases, and for heaven's sake do not bother him.' Maude who had her own lover, and was perfectly satisfied with him though she had been engaged to him for nearly twelve months, knew that things were not going well, and was unhappy. But at the moment she said nothing further.

'Where is this recreant knight?' said Francesca. There was something in the tone of Miss Altifiorla's voice which grated against Cecilia's ears, and almost made her angry. But she knew that in her present condition it behoved her to be especially careful. Had she resolved to break

13

with her betrothed she would have been quite open on the subject to all her friends. She would have been open to all Exeter. But in her present condition of mind she was resolved, — she thought she was resolved, — to go on with her marriage.

'Why you should call him a recreant knight, I cannot for the life of me understand,' she said. 'But it seems that Sir Francis, who is not exactly in his first youth, is supposed to be as attentive as a young turtle dove.'

'I always used to think,' said Miss Altifiorla gravely, 'that a gentleman was bound to keep his promise.'

'Oh heavens, how grave you all are! A gentleman and his promise! Do you mean to assert that Sir Francis is no gentleman, and does not keep his promises? Because if so I shall be angry.' Then there was an end of that conversation.

But she was stirred to absolute anger by what took place with Mrs Green, though she was unable to express her anger. Mrs Green's manner to her had always been that of a somewhat humble friend, — of one who lived in lodgings in the High Street, and who accepted dinners without returning them. And since this engagement with Sir Francis had become a fact, her manner had become perhaps a little more humble. She used to say of herself that of course she was poor; of course she had nothing to give. Her husband was only a Minor Canon, and had married her, alas, without a fortune. It is not to be supposed that on this account Cecilia was inclined to ill-treat her friend; but the way of the world is such. People are taken and must be taken in the position they frame for themselves. Mrs Green was Cecilia Holt's humble friend, and as such was expected to be humble. When, therefore, she volunteered a little advice to Cecilia about her lover, it was not taken altogether in good part. 'My dear Cecilia,' she said, 'I do really think that you ought to say something to Sir Francis.'

'Say something!' answered Cecilia sharply. 'What am I to say? I say everything to him that comes in his way.'

'I think, my dear, he is just a little inattentive. I have gone through it all, and of course know what it means. It is not that he is deficient in love, but that he allows a hundred little things to stand in his way.'

'What nonsense you do talk!'

'But, my dear, you see I have gone through it all myself, and I do know what I am talking about.'

'Mr Green — ! Do you mean to liken Mr Green to Sir Francis?'

'They are both gentlemen,' said Mrs Green with a slight tone of anger. 'And though Sir Francis is a baronet, Mr Green is a clergyman.'

'My dear Bessy, you know that is not what I meant. In that respect they are both alike. But you, when you were engaged, were about three years younger than the man, and I am nearly twenty years younger than Sir Francis. You don't suppose that I can put myself altogether on the same platform with him as you did with your lover. It is absurd to suppose it. Do you let him go his way, and me go mine. You may be sure that not a word of reproach will ever fall from my lips.' — 'Till we are married,' Cecilia had intended to say, but she did not complete the sentence.

But the words of her comforters had their effect, as no doubt was the case with Job. She had complained to no one, but everybody had seen her condition. Her poor dear old mother, who would have put up with a very moderate amount of good usage on the part of such a lover as Sir Francis, had been aware that things were not as they should be. Her three friends, to whom she had not opened her mouth in the way of expressing her grievance, had all seen her trouble. That Maude Hippesley and Miss Altifiorla had noticed it did not strike her with much surprise, but that Mrs Green should have expressed herself so boldly was startling. She could not but turn the matter over in her own mind and ask herself whether she were ill-treated. And it was not only those differences which the ladies noticed which struck her as ominous, but a certain way which Sir Francis had when talking to herself which troubled her. That light tone of contempt if begun now would certainly not be dropped after their marriage. He had assumed an easy way of almost laughing at her, of quizzing her pursuits, and, worse still, of only half listening to her, which she felt to promise very badly for her future happiness. If he wanted his liberty he should have it, — now and then. She would never be a drag on her husband's happiness. She had resolved from the very first not to be an exigeant wife. She would care for all his cares, but she would never be a troublesome wife. All that had been matter of deep thought to her. And if he were not given to literary tastes in earnest, — for in the first days of their love-making there had been, as was natural, a little pretence, — she would not harass him by her pursuits. And she would sympathise with his racing and his shooting. And she would interest herself, if possible, about Newmarket, — as to which place she found he had a taste. And, joined to all the rest, there came a conviction that his real tastes did take that direction. She had never before heard that he had a passion for the turf; but if it should turn out that he was a gambler! Had any of her friends mentioned such an idea to her a week ago, how she would have rebuked that friend! But now she added this to her other grievances, and began to tell herself that she had become engaged to a man whom she did not know and whom she already doubted.

Then there came a week of very troubled existence, — of existence the more troubled because she had no one to whom to tell of her trouble. As to putting confidence in her mother, — that idea never occurred to her. Her mother among her friends was the humblest of all. To tell her mother that she was going to be married was a matter of course, but she had never consulted her mother on the subject. And now, at the end of the week, she had almost resolved to break with the man without having intimated to anyone that such was her intention. And what excuse had she? There was excuse enough to her own mind, to her own heart. But what excuse could she give to him or to the world? He was confident enough, — so confident as to vex her by his confidence. Though he had come to treat her with indifference, like a plaything, she was quite sure that he did not dream of having his marriage broken off. He was secured, — she was sure that this was his feeling, — by her love, by her ambition, by his position in the world. He could make her Lady Geraldine! Was it to be supposed that she should not wish to be Lady Geraldine? He could take what liberties he pleased without any danger of losing her! It was her conviction that such was the condition of his mind that operated the strongest in bringing her to her resolution.

But she must tell someone. She must have a confidante. 'Maude,' she said one day, 'I have made up my mind not to marry your uncle.'

'Cecilia!'

'I have. No one as yet has been told, but I have resolved. Should I see him to-morrow, or next day, or the next, I shall tell him.'

'You are not in earnest?'

'Is it likely that I should jest on such a subject; — or that if I had a mind to do so I should tell you? You must keep my secret. You must not tell your uncle. It must come to him from myself. At the present moment he does not in the least know me, — but he will.'

'And why? Why is there to be this break; — why to be these broken promises?'

'I put it to yourself whether you do not know the why. How often have you made excuses for him? Why have the excuses been necessary? I am prepared to bear all the blame. I must bear it. But I am not prepared to make myself miserable for ever because I have made a mistake as to a man's character. Of course I shall suffer, — because I love him. He will not suffer much, — because he does not love me.'

'Oh, yes!'

'You know that he does not,' said Cecilia, shaking her head. 'You know it. You know it. At any rate I know it. And as the thing has to be done, it shall be done quickly.' There was much more said between the two girls on the subject, but Maude when she left her friend was sure that her friend was in earnest.

Chapter II

SIR FRANCIS GERALDINE

On that same afternoon, at about tea-time, Sir Francis came up to the house. He had said that he would be there if he could get there, — and he got there. He was shown into the drawing-room, where was sitting Mrs Holt with her daughter, and began to tell them that he was to leave the Deanery on the following morning and not be back till a day or two before his marriage. 'Where are you going?' Cecilia asked, meaning nothing, only gaining time till she should have determined how she should carry out her purpose.

'Well; — if you must know, I am going to Goodwood. I had not thought of it. But some friends have reminded me that as these are to be the last days of my liberty I may as well enjoy them.'

'Your friends are very complaisant to me,' said Cecilia in a tone of voice which seemed to imply, that she took it all in earnest.

'One's friends never do care a straw for the young lady on such an occasion,' said Sir Francis. 'They regard her as the conquering enemy, and him as the conquered victim.'

'And you desire a little relaxation from your fetters.'

'Well; just a last flutter.' All this had been said

with such a mixture of indifferent badinage on his part, and of serious anger on hers, that Mrs Holt, who saw it all and understood it, sat very uneasy in her chair. 'To tell the truth,' continued he, 'all the instructions have been given to the lawyers, and I really do think, that I had better be away during the making of the dresses and the baking of the cake. It has come to pass by this accident of my living at the Deanery that we have already become almost tired of each other's company.'

'You might speak for yourself, Sir Francis Geraldine.'

'So I do. For to tell the truth a man does get tired of this kind of thing quicker than a woman, and a man of forty much quicker than a woman of twenty. At any rate I'm off to-morrow.'

There was something in the tone of all this which thoroughly confirmed her in her purpose. There should come an end to him of his thraldom. This should not be by many the last of his visits to Goodwood. He should never again have to complain of the trouble given to him by her company. She sat silent, turning it all over in her mind, and struggling to think how she might best get her mother out of the room. She must do it instantly; — now at once. She was perfectly resolved that he should not leave that house an engaged man. But she did not see her direct way to the commencement of the difficult conversation. 'Mrs Holt,' said Sir Francis, 'don't you think a little absence will be best for both of us, before

21

we begin the perilous voyage of matrimony to-gether?'

'I'm sure I don't know,' said poor Mrs Holt.

'There can't be a doubt about it,' continued the lover. 'I have become so stupid, that I hardly know how to put one foot before the other, and Cecilia is so majestical that her dignity is growing to be almost tedious.'

'Mamma,' said Cecilia after a pause, 'as Sir Francis is going to-morrow, would you mind leaving us alone for a few minutes. There is something which I have to say to him.'

'Oh, certainly, my dear,' said Mrs Holt as she got up and left the room.

Now had come the moment, the difficult moment in which Cecilia Holt had to remodel for herself the course of her future life. For the last month or two she had been the affianced bride of a baronet, and of a man of fashion. All Exeter had known her as the future Lady Geraldine. And more than that, she had learned to regard herself as the owner of the man, and of his future home. Her imagination had been active in drawing pictures for herself of the life she was to live, — pictures which for a time had been rosy-hued. But whatever the tints may have been, and how far the bright colours may have become dimmed, it had been as Lady Geraldine, and not as Cecilia Holt, that she had looked in the glass which had shown to herself her future career. Now, within the last four-and-twenty hours, — for the last crowning purpose of her resolution was hardly of longer date, — she had determined to alter it all. But he as yet did not know it. He still regarded her as his affianced bride. Now had come the moment in which the truth must be told to him.

As soon as her mother left the room, she got up from her seat, as did also her lover. He, as soon as the door was closed, at once attempted to put his arm round the girl's waist, as was his undoubted privilege. She with the gentlest possible motion rejected his embrace and contrived to stand at a little distance from him. But she said nothing. The subject to be discussed was so difficult that words would not come to her assistance. Then he lent her his aid. 'You do not mean that you're in a tiff because of what I said just now. Of course it is better that we should not be together for the few days before our marriage.'

'I do not think that I am in a tiff, Sir Francis. I hope I am not, because what I have to say is too serious for ill humour.' Then she paused. 'What I have got to say is of some importance; — of very great importance. Sir Francis Geraldine, I feel that I have to ask you to forgive me.'

'What on earth is the matter?'

'You may well ask. And, indeed, I do not know how to excuse myself. Your friends will say that I am frivolous, and vain, and discontented.'

'What the mischief is it all about?' he demanded with an angry voice.

She knew she had not as yet told him. She

could perceive that he had not gathered from her first words any inkling of the truth; and yet she did not know how to tell him. If it were once told she could, she thought, defend herself. But the difficulty was to find the words by which she could let him know what was her intention. 'Sir Francis, I fear that we have misunderstood each other.'

'How misunderstood? Why Sir Francis? Am I to understand that you want to quarrel with me because I am going away? If so speak it out. I shall go just the same.'

'Your going has no bearing upon my present purpose. I had made up my mind before I had heard of your going; — only when I did hear of it it became necessary that I should tell you at once.'

'But you have told me nothing. I hate mysteries, and secrets, and scenes. There is nothing goes against the grain so much with me as tragedy airs. If you have done anything amiss that it is necessary that I should know let me know it at once.' As he said this there came across his brow a look of anger and of hot ill-humour, such as she had never seen there before. The effect was to induce her to respect him rather than to be afraid of him. It was well that a man should have the power and the courage to show his anger.

But it encouraged her to proceed with her task. She certainly was not afraid of him personally, though she did dread what the world might say of her, and especially what might be said by his friends. 'I do not know that I have done anything amiss of which I need tell you,' she said with quiet dignity. 'It is rather that which I intend to do. I fear, Sir Francis, that you and I have made a mistake in this.'

'What mistake?' he shouted. 'While you beat about the bush I shall never understand you.'

'In our proposed marriage.'

'What?'

'I fear that I should not make you happy.'

'What on earth do you mean?' Then he paused a moment before he continued, which he did as though he had discovered suddenly the whole secret. 'You have got another lover.'

There was something in the idea so shocking to Cecilia, so revolting, — so vulgar in the mode of expression, that the feeling at once gave her the strength necessary to go on with her task. She would not condescend to answer the accusation, but at once told her story in plain language. 'I think, Sir Francis Geraldine, that you do not feel for me the regard that would make me happy as your wife. Do not interrupt me just at present,' she said, stopping him, as some exclamation was escaping from his lips. 'Hear me to the end, and if you have aught to say, I will then hear you. Of my own regard for you I will say nothing. But I think that I have been mistaken as to your nature. In fact, I feel sure that we are neither of us that which the other supposed. It is lamentable that we should have fallen into such an error, but it is well that even yet we can escape from it before it is too late. As my mind is altogether made up, I can only ask your pardon for what I have done to you, expressing myself sure at the same time I am now best consulting your future happiness.'

During this last speech of Cecilia's, Sir Francis had sat down, while she still stood in her old place. He had seated himself on the sofa, assuming as it were a look of profound ease, and arranging the nails of one hand with the fingers of the other, as though he were completely indifferent to the words spoken to him. 'Have you done yet?' he said as soon as she was silent.

'Yes, I have done.'

'And you are sure that if I begin you will not interrupt me till I have done?'

'I think not, — if there be aught that you have to say.'

'Well, considering that ten minutes since I was engaged to make you Lady Geraldine, and that now I am supposed to be absolved from any such necessity, I presume you will think it expedient that I should say something. I suppose that I have not been told the whole truth.' Then he stopped, as though in spite of his injunction as to her silence, he expected an answer from her. But she made none, though there came a cloud of anger upon her face. 'I suppose, I say, that there is something of which it is not considered necessary that I should be informed. There must be something of the kind, or you would hardly abandon prospects which a few days since appeared to you to be so desirable.'

'I have not thought it necessary to speak of your temper,' she said.

'Nor of your own.'

'Nor of my own,' she added.

'But there is, I take it, something beyond that. I do not think that my temper, bad as it may be, — nor your own, — would have sufficed to estrange you. There must be something more palpable than temper to have occasioned it. And though you have not thought fit to tell me, you must feel that my position justifies me in asking. Have you another lover?'

'No,' she exclaimed, burning with wrath, but with head so turned from him that he should not see her.

'Nor have ever had one? I am entitled to ask the question, though perhaps I should have asked it before.'

'You are at any rate not entitled to ask it now. Sir Francis Geraldine, between you and me all is over. I can only beg you to understand most positively that all is over.'

'My dear Miss Holt, you need not insist upon that, as it is perfectly understood.'

'Then there need be no further words. If I have done you any wrong I ask your pardon. You have wronged me only in your thoughts. I must take what consolation I can from the feeling that the injury will fall chiefly upon my head and not upon yours.' Then without a further word of farewell she marched out of the room.

Sir Francis, when he found himself alone,

shook himself, as it were, as he rose from the sofa, and looked about the room in amazement. It was quite true that she was gone — gone, as far as he was concerned, for ever. It did not occur to him for a moment that there could be any reconciliation between them, and his first feeling undoubtedly was one of amazed disappointment. Then, standing there in Mrs Holt's drawing-room, he began to bethink himself what could have been the cause of it. Since the first week of his engagement he had begun and had continued to tell himself what great things he was about to do for Cecilia Holt. With her beauty, her grace, her dignity and her accomplishments, he was quite satisfied. It was expedient that he should marry, and he did not know that he could marry much better. Cecilia, when her mother died, would have twenty thousand pounds, and that in his eyes had been sufficient. But he was about to make her Lady Geraldine, and the more that he thought of this, the more grateful it had appeared to him that she should be to him. Then by degrees, as he had expected from her expressions of gratitude, she had rebelled against him. Of the meaning of this he had not been quite conscious, but had nevertheless felt it necessary that he should dominate her spirit. Up to the moment in which this interview had begun he had thought that he was learning to do so. She had not dared to ask him questions which would have been so natural, or to demand from him services to which she was entitled. It was thus that he had regarded her conduct. But he had never feared for a moment but that he was on the road to success. Up to the moment at which he had entered the room he had thought that he was progressing favourably. His Cecilia was becoming tame in his hands, as was necessary. He had then been altogether taken aback and surprised by her statement to him, and could not for some moments get over his feeling of amazement. At last he uttered a low whistle, and then walked slowly out of the house. At the front door he found his horse, and mounting it, rode back into Exeter. As he did so he began to inquire of himself whether this step which the girl had determined to take was really a misfortune to him or the reverse. He had hardly as yet asked himself any such question since the day on which he had first become engaged to her. He had long thought of marrying, and one girl after another had been rejected by him as he had passed them in review through his thoughts. Then had come Cecilia's turn, and she had seemed to answer the purpose. There had been about her an especial dignity which had suited his views of matrimonial life. She was a young woman as to whom all his friends would say that he had done well in marrying her. But by degrees there had come upon him a feeling of the general encumbrance of a wife. Would she not interfere with him? Would she not wish to hinder him when he chose to lead a bachelor's life? Newmarket for instance, and his London clubs, and his fishing in

Norway, — would she not endeavour to set her foot upon them? Would it not be well that he should teach her that she would not be allowed to interfere? He had therefore begun to teach her — and this had come of it! It had been quite unexpected, but still he felt as though he were released from a burden.

He had accused her of having had another lover. At the moment an idea had passed through his mind that she was suddenly prompted by her conscience to tell him something that she had hitherto concealed. There had been some lover, probably, as to whom every one had been silent to him. He was a jealous man, and for a moment he had been hurt. He would have said that his heart had been hurt. There was but little of heart in it, for it may be doubted whether he had ever loved her. But there was something pricked him which filled him for the instant with serious thoughts. When he had asked the question he wished to see her at his feet. There had come no answer, and he told himself that he was justified in thinking the surmise to be true. He was justified to himself, but only for the moment, for at the next had come her declaration that all was to be over between them. The idea of the lover became buried under the ruins which were thus made.

So she intended to escape from him! But he also would escape from her. After all, what an infinite trouble would a wife be to him, — especially a wife of whose docility in harness he was

30

not quite assured. But there came upon him as he rode home an idea that the world would say that he had been jilted. Of course he would have been jilted, but there would be nothing in that except as the world might speak of it. It was gall to him to have to think that the world of Exeter should believe that Cecilia Holt had changed her mind, and had sent him about his business. If the world of Exeter would say that he had ill-used the girl, and had broken off the engagement for mere fancy, — as she had done, — that would be much more endurable. He could not say that such was the case. To so palpable a lie the contradiction would be easy and disgraceful. But could he not so tell the story as to leave a doubt on the minds of the people? That question of another lover had not been contradicted. Thinking of it again as he rode home he began to feel that the lover must be true, and that her conduct in breaking off the engagement had been the consequence. There had been some complication in the way of which she had been unable to rid herself; at any rate it was quite out of the question that he should have held himself to such an engagement, complicated as it would have been with such a lover. There would be some truth, therefore, in so telling the story as to leave the matter in doubt, and in doubt he resolved that he would leave it. Before he got back to the Deanery he was, he thought, thoroughly glad that he should have been enabled so easily to slip his neck out of the collar.

Chapter III

THE END
OF THAT EPISODE

Cecilia during the following day told no one what had occurred, nor on the morning of the next. Indeed she did not open her mouth on the subject till Maude Hippesley came to her. She felt that she was doing wrong to her mother by keeping her in the dark, but she could not bring herself to tell it. She had, as she now declared to herself, settled the question of her future life. To live with her mother, — and then to live alone, must be her lot. She had been accustomed, before the coming of Sir Francis, to speak of this as a thing certain; but then it had not been certain, had not been probable, even to her own mind. Of course lovers would come till the acceptable lover should be accepted. The threats of a single life made by pretty girls with good fortunes never go for much in this world. Then in due time the acceptable lover had come, and had been accepted.

And to what purpose had she put him? She could not even now say of what she accused him, having rejected him. What excuse could she give? What answer could she allege? She was more sure than ever now that she could not live with him as his wife. He had said words about some former lover which were not the less painful, in that there had been no foundation for

32

them. There had in truth been nothing for her to tell Sir Francis Geraldine. Out of her milk-white innocency no confession was to be made. But what there was had all been laid bare to him. There had been no lover, — but if there had, then there would have been a lie told. She had said that there had been none, and he had heard her assertion with those greedy ears which men sometimes have for such telling. It was a comfort to him that there had been none; and when something uncomfortable came in his way he immediately thought that she had deceived him. She must bear with all that now. It did not much matter, she assured herself, what he might think of her. But for the moment she could hardly endure to think of it, much less to talk of it. She did not know how to own to her mother that she was simply a jilt without offering anything in excuse. The truth must be told, but, oh, how bitter must the truth be! Even that accusation as to the lover had not been made till after she had resolved to reject him; and she could not bring herself to lie to her mother by pretending that the one had caused the other.

After lunch on the second day Maude Hippesley came down and found her amongst the trees in the shrubbery. It will be remembered that Maude was niece to Sir Francis, and was at the present time living in the same house with him. 'Cecilia,' she said, 'what is this that has happened?'

'He has told you then?'

'What is it? He has told us all that you have quarrelled, and now he has gone away.'

'Thank God for that!'

'Yes, — he has gone. But he told us only just as he went. And he has made a mystery of it, — so that I do not know how it has happened, — or why.'

'Did I not tell you?'

'Yes, — you told me something, — something that made me think you mad. But it is he that has rejected you now!'

'Has he told you that?'

'He has told us all so just as he was leaving us. After his things were packed up he told us.' Cecilia stood still and looked into her friend's face. Maude she knew could say nothing to her that was not true. 'He has made a mystery of it, but that has been the impression he has left upon us. At any rate there has been a quarrel.'

'Yes; — there has been a quarrel.'

'And now our only business is to make it up. It is impossible that two people who have loved each other as you have done should be allowed to part in so absurd a manner. It is like two children who think they are never to be friends again because of some momentary disagreement.' Maude Hippesley, who had not lived in the same town with her lover and therefore had never quarrelled with him, was awfully wise. 'It is quite out of the question,' she continued, 'that this thing should go on. I don't think it matters in the least whether you quarrel with him or he with you. But of course you must make it up. And as you are the woman it is only proper that you should begin.'

How much had Cecilia to do before she could prove to her friend that no such beginning was possible. In the first place there was the falsehood, the base falsehood, which Sir Francis had told. In order to save himself he had declared that he had rejected her. It was very mean. At this moment its peculiar meanness made her feel doubly sure that the man was altogether unfitted to be her husband. But she would allow the false assertion to pass unnoticed. If he could find a comfort in that let him have it. Perhaps upon the whole it would be better that some story should go forth in Exeter. It could not be told by her because it was untrue; but for the moment she thought that she might pass it by without notice. 'There can be no fresh beginning,' she said. 'We two have already come to the end of all that is likely to take place between us. Dear Maude, pray do not trouble me. No doubt as time goes by we shall talk of it all again. But just at present, circumstanced as you are with him, nothing but silence between you and me can be fitting. I hope that you and I at any rate will never quarrel.'

After that she told her mother and her two other friends. Her mother was for a week or two in despair. She endeavoured by means of the family at the Deanery to bring about some reconciliation. The Dean, who did not in truth like his brother-in-law and was a little afraid of him, altogether refused to interfere in the matter. Mrs Hippesley was of opinion that the lovers would be sure to 'come round' if left to themselves. Maude who, though she had not liked her uncle, had thought much of his position and had been proud of the idea that he should marry an Exeter girl and her own peculiar friend, was in despair. But the Deanery collectively refused to take active steps in the matter. Mrs Green was of opinion that Cecilia must have behaved badly. There had been some affair of pride in which she had declined to give way. According to Mrs Green's ideas a woman could hardly yield too much to a man before marriage, so as to secure him in order that her time for management might come afterwards. With Miss Altifiorla, Cecilia found for awhile more comfort; but even from this noted hater of the other sex the comfort was not exactly of the kind she wanted. Miss Altifiorla was of opinion that men on the whole are bad, but seemed to think that among men this baronet was not a bad specimen. He did not want a great deal of attention and was fairly able to get about by himself without calling upon his future wife to be always with him. Then he had a title and an income and a house; and was in short one of those who are in a measure compelled to marry. Miss Altifiorla thought it a pity that the match should be broken off, but was quite ready to console her friend as to the misfortune.

There was one point as to which Cecilia was

quite decided, and in this Miss Altifiorla bore
her out altogether. That question of marriage
was now settled once and for ever. Cecilia, much
in opposition to her friend's wishes, had tried
her hand at it and had failed. She had fallen
grievously to the ground and had bruised herself
dreadfully in making the attempt. It had perhaps
been necessary, as Miss Altifiorla thought. It is
not given to all to know their own strength as it
had been given to her. They had often discussed
these matters and Miss Altifiorla had always
been very firm. So had Cecilia been firm; — but
then she had given way, had broken down, had
consented to regard herself as a mere woman
and no stronger than other women. She had
given herself to a man in order that she might be
the mother of his children and the head servant
in his household. She had shown herself to be
false for the moment to her great principles. But
Providence had intervened. It may be surmised
that Miss Altifiorla in discussing the matter with
herself did not use the word Providence. Nor
was it Chance. And as the rejection had come
from the gentleman's hands, — so Miss
Altifiorla was taught to believe, — she could not
boast that Cecilia had accomplished it. But some
mysterious agency had been at work which
would not permit so exceptional a young lady as
Miss Holt to fall into the common quagmire of
marriage. She had escaped, — thanks to the
mysterious agency, and must be doubly, trebly,
armed with resolution lest she should stumble

again. 'I think,' she said one day to Cecilia, 'I think that you have great cause to be thankful that he should have repented of his bargain before it was too late.'

Flesh is flesh after all and human nature no stronger than human nature. Cecilia had consented to bear in silence the idea that she had been jilted, and had endured her mother's tender little sympathies on the subject. But there was a difficulty to her in suffering this direct statement from her friend. Why would not her friend let the matter be passed by in silence! 'It is well,' she said, 'that we both repented.'

Now the subject had been much discussed in Exeter, — whether Sir Francis had jilted Miss Holt or Miss Holt Sir Francis. It had been always present to Miss Hippesley's mind, that her friend had told her of her intention at a time when she was quite sure that Sir Francis had no such notion in his head. And when, on the day but one following, she had told Cecilia of the statement which Sir Francis had made at the Deanery, Cecilia had not contradicted it, but had expressed her surprise. She therefore had resolved to decide the question against her uncle, and had given rise to the party who were on that side. But the outside world were strongly of opinion that Sir Francis had been the first offender. It was so much the more probable. Miss Altifiorla had always taken that side, and had spoken everywhere of him as the great sinner. Still however there was a doubt in her own mind, as to which she was desirous of receiving such solution as Cecilia could give her. She was determined now to push the question. 'But,' said she, 'I suppose it originated with him? It is a great thing for us to feel that you have not been to blame at all in the matter.'

'I have been to blame,' said Cecilia.

'But how? The man comes here and proposes himself; and is accepted, and then breaks away from his engagement without reason and without excuse. It is a thing to be thankful for, that he should have done so; but we have also to be thankful that the fault has not been on our side.' Miss Altifiorla had almost brought herself to believe that the man had made love to her, and proposed to her, that she in a moment of weakness had accepted him, and that she now had been luckily saved by his inconstancy.

'I think we will drop that part of the question,' said Miss Holt, showing by her manner that she did not choose to be cross-questioned. 'In such cases there is generally fault on both sides.' Then there was nothing further said on the subject, but Miss Altifiorla pondered much over her friend's weakness in not being able to confess that she had been jilted.

All this had happened in the summer. During the gala days of the projected wedding plans had been made of course for the honeymoon. Sir Francis with his bride were to go here and to go there, and poor Mrs Holt had been fated to remain at home as though no arrangement had been necessary for her happiness. Indeed none had been necessary. She was quite content to remain at Exeter and expect such excitement as might come to her from letters from Lady Geraldine. To talk to everybody around her about Lady Geraldine would have sufficed for her. And when all these hopes were broken up and it had been really decided that there should be no wedding, — when it became apparent that Cecilia Holt was to remain as Cecilia Holt, still there was no autumn tour. Cecilia had declared that in no place would life be so quiet for her as at home. 'Mamma,' she had said, 'let us prepare ourselves for what is to come. You and I mean to live together happily, and our life must be a home life!' Then she applied herself specially to the flowers and the shrubs, and began even to look after the vegetables in the fullness of her energy. In these days she did not see much of her three friends. In August Maude was married and became Mrs Thorne. Mr Thorne was the eldest son of a Squire from Honiton for whom things were to be made modestly comfortable during his father's life. Maude's coming marriage had not been counted as much during the days of her friend's high hopes, but had risen in consideration since the fall which had taken place. Between Miss Altifiorla and Cecilia there had come, not a quarrel, but a coolness. The two ladies did continue to see each other occasionally, but there was but little between them to console misery. Miss Altifiorla had attempted to

40

resume her position of equality, — unreasoned and imaginary equality, — with perhaps a slight step in advance to which in their present circumstances she was entitled by their age. Cecilia cared nothing for equality, but would not consent to be held to have lost anything. Though Miss Altifiorla declared that her friend had risen very highly in her sentiments, there was too evidently a depreciation in her manner; and this Cecilia could not endure. Consequently the two ladies were not, at this period, of much comfort one to the other. With Mrs Green matters might have been different; but Mrs Green too manifestly thought that Cecilia had been wrong, and still clung to the idea that with proper management the baronet might be made to come back again. With a lady holding such ideas as these there could be no sympathy.

In owning the truth it must be confessed that Cecilia at this period of her life was too self-conscious. She did not think, but felt, that the world all around her was suffused by a Holt-Geraldine aspect and flavour. She could not walk abroad without an idea that the people whom she saw were talking about her. She could not shut herself in her garden without a conviction that the passersby were saying that the girl living there had been jilted by Sir Francis Geraldine. She had been well aware of the greatness of the position in which she was to have been placed; and though she had abandoned the situation without a doubt as soon as she had learned her mistake as to the man's character, still she felt the fall, and inwardly grieved over it. She had not known herself at first, — how grievous would be her isolation when she found herself alone. Such was the case with her now, so that she fretted and made herself ill. By degrees she confined herself more and more to the house, till her mother seeing it, interfered. She became sick, captious, and querulous. The old family doctor interfered and advised that she should be taken away from Exeter. 'For ever?' asked Mrs Holt. The doctor did not say for ever. Mrs Holt might probably be able to let the house for a year and go elsewhere for that period. Then there arose questions as to all the pretty furniture, and their household goods. Cecilia herself was most unwilling. But before Christmas came, arrangements had been made, and the house was let, and the first of January saw Mrs Holt and her daughter comfortably established in a pension at Nice. Mrs Holt at any rate declared that she was comfortable, though Cecilia on her mother's behalf, stated it to be impossible. She herself told herself, — though she had whispered no word on the subject to living ears, — she herself told herself that she had been driven abroad by the falsehood which Sir Francis had told. She could not bear to live in Exeter as the girl that had been jilted.

This is the episode in the life of Cecilia Holt which it is necessary should be first told.

Chapter IV

MR WESTERN

The Holts travelled about during the whole of that year, passing the summer in Switzerland and the autumn in the north of Italy, and found themselves at Rome in November, with the intention of remaining there for the winter. One place was the same to them as another, and it was necessary that they should at any rate exist until the term had expired for which they had let their house. Mrs Holt had I think enjoyed her life. She had been made more of than at home, and had been happy amidst the excitement. But with Cecilia it had been for many months as though all things had been made of leather and prunello. She had not cared, or had not seemed to care, for scenery or for cities. In that last episode of her life she had aspired to a new career, and had at first been fairly successful. And she had loved the man honestly for a time, and had buoyed herself up with great intentions as to the future duties of her life. Then had come her downfall, in which it was commonly said of her that she had been jilted by her lover. Even when the mountains of Switzerland had been so fine before her eyes as in truth to console her by their beauty, she had not admitted that she was consoled. The Campanile at Florence had filled her with that satisfaction which comes from supreme beauty. But still when she went home to her hotel she thought more of Sir Francis Geraldine than of the Campanile. To have been jilted would be bad, but to have it said of her that she had been jilted when she was conscious that it was untrue was a sore provocation. And yet no one could say but that she had behaved well and been instigated by good motives. She had found that her lover was ignoble, and did not love her. And she had at once separated herself from him. And since that in all her correspondence with her friends she had quietly endured the idea which would continually crop up that she had been jilted. She never denied it; but it was the false accusation rather than the loss of all that her marriage had promised her which made her feel the Matterhorn and the Campanile to be equally ineffective. Then there gradually came to her some comfort from a source from which she had certainly not expected it. On their travels they had become acquainted with a Mr Western, a silent, shy, almost middle-aged man, whom they had sat next to at dinner for nearly a week before they had become acquainted with him. But they had passed on from scenery to city, and, as had been their fortune, Mr Western had passed on with them. Who does not know the way in which some strange traveller becomes his friend on a second or a third meeting in some station or hotel saloon? In this way Mrs Holt and Cecilia had become acquainted with Mr Western, and on parting with him at Venice in October had received with gratification the assurance that he would again 'turn up' in Rome.

'He is a very good sort of man,' said Mrs Holt to her daughter that night. Cecilia agreed, but with perhaps less enthusiasm than her mother had displayed. For Mrs Holt the assertion had been quite enthusiastic. But Cecilia did think that Mr Western had made himself agreeable. He was an unmarried man, however, and there had been something in the nature of a communication which he had made to her, that had prevented her from being loud in his praise. Not that the communication had been one which had in any way given offense; but it had been unexpected, confidential, and of such a nature as to create much thought. No doubt an intimacy had sprung up between them. But yet it was singular that a man apparently so reticent as Mr Western should make such a communication. How the intimacy had grown by degrees need not here be explained, but that it had grown to be very close will appear from the nature of the story told.

The story was one of Mr Western's own life and was as follows. He was a man of good but not of large private means. He had been to Oxford and had there distinguished himself. He had been called to the bar but had not practised. He had gone into Parliament, but had left it, finding that the benches of the House of Commons were only fitted for the waste of time. He had joined scientific societies to which he still belonged, but which he did not find to be sufficient for his happiness. During these attempts and changes he had taken a house in London, and having a house had thought it well to look for a wife. He had become engaged to a certain Miss Mary Tremenhere, and by her he had been — jilted. Since that, for twelve months he had been travelling abroad in quest, he said, not of consolation, but of some mitigation of his woe. Cecilia, when she heard this, whispered to him one little question, 'Do you love her?' 'I thought I did,' he answered. And then the subject was dropped.

It was a most singular communication for him to make. Why should he, an elderly man as she at first took him to be, select her as the recipient for such a tale? She took him to be an elderly man, till she found by the accidents of conversation that he was two years younger than Sir Francis Geraldine. Then she looked into his face and saw that that appearance of age had come upon him from sorrow. There was a tinge of grey through his hair, and there were settled lines about his face, and a look of steadied thought about his mouth, which robbed him of all youth. But when she observed his upright form, and perceived that he was a strong stalwart man, in the very pride of manhood as far as strength was concerned, — then she felt that she had wronged him. Still he was one who had suffered so much as to be entitled to be called old. She felt the impossibility of putting him in the same category among men as that filled by Sir Francis Geraldine. The strength of manhood was still there, but not the salt of youth. But why should he have told her, — her who had exactly the same story to tell back again, if only she could tell it? Once, twice there came to her an idea that she would tell it. He had sought for sympathy, not under the assurance of secrecy but with the full conviction as she felt it, that his secret would be safe. Why should not she do the same? That there would be great comfort in doing so she was well aware. To have some one who would sympathise with her! Hitherto she had no one. Even her mother, who was kindness, even obedience itself, who attended to her smallest wish, even her mother regretted the baronet son-in-law. 'And yet she would have been left all alone,' she said to herself, marvelling at the unselfish fondness of a mother. Mr Western would be bound to sympathise. Having called upon her for sympathy, his must be ready. But when she had thought of it thrice she did not do it. Were she to tell her story it would seem as though she were repeating to him back his own. 'I too have been in love, and engaged, and have jilted a gentleman considerably my senior in age.' She would have to say that, likening herself to the girl who had jilted him, — or else to tell the other story, the untrue story, the story which the world believed, in order that she might be on a par with him. This she could not do. If she told any she must tell the truth, and the truth was not suitable to be told. Therefore she kept her peace, and sympathised with a one-sided sympathy.

In Rome they did again meet, and on this occasion they met as quite old friends. He called upon them at their hotel and sat with them, happier than usual in his manner, and, for him, almost light and gay of heart. Parties were made to St Peter's, and the Coliseum, and the Capitol. When he left on that occasion Cecilia remarked to her mother how much less triste he was than usual. 'Men, I suppose,' she said to herself, 'get over that kind of thing quicker than women.'

In Rome it seemed to Cecilia that Mr Western when alone with her had no other subject for conversation than the ill treatment he had received from Mary Tremenhere. His eagerness in coming back to the subject quite surprised her. She herself was fascinated by it, but yet felt it would be better were she to put a stop to it. There was no way of doing this unless she were to take her mother from Rome. She could not tell him that on that matter he had said enough, nor could she warn him that so much of confidential intercourse between them would give rise in the minds of others to erroneous ideas. Her mother never seemed to see that there was anything peculiar in their intercourse. And so it went on from day to day and from week to week.

'You asked me once whether I loved her,' he said one day. 'I did; but I am astonished now that it should have been so. She was very lovely.'

'I suppose so.'

'The most perfect complexion that was ever seen on a lady's cheek.' Cecilia remembered that her complexion too had been praised before this blow had fallen upon her. 'The colour would come and go so rapidly that I used to marvel what were the thoughts that drove the blood hither and thither. There were no thoughts, — unless of her own prettiness and her own fortunes. She accepted me as a husband because it was necessary for her to settle in life. I was in Parliament, and that she thought to be something. I had a house in Chester Square, and that was something. She was promised a carriage, and that conquered her. As the bride I had chosen for myself she became known to many, and then she began to understand that she might have done better with herself. I am old, and not given to many amusements. Then came a man with a better income and with fewer years; and she did not hesitate for a moment. When she took me aside and told me that she had changed her mind, it was her quiescence and indifference that disturbed me most. There was nothing of her new lover; but simply that she did not love me. I did not stoop for a moment to a prayer. I took her at her word, and left her. Within a week she was acknowledged to be engaged to Captain Geraldine.'

The naming of the name of course struck Cecilia Holt. She remembered to have heard something of the coming marriage by her lover's cousin, and something, too, of the story of the girl. But it had reached her ear in the lightest form, and had hardly remained in her memory.

It was now of no matter, as she had determined to keep her own history to herself. Therefore she made no exclamation when the name of Geraldine was mentioned.

'How could I love her after that?' he continued, betraying the strong passion which he felt. 'I had loved a girl whose existence I had imagined, and of whom I had seen merely the outward form, and had known nothing of the inner self. What is it that we love?' he continued. 'Is it merely the coloured doll, soft to touch and pleasant to kiss? Or is it some inner nature which we hope to discover, and of which we have found the outside so attractive? I had found no inner self which it had been possible that I could love. He was welcome to the mere doll who was wanted simply that she should grace his equipage. I have asked myself, Why is it that I am so sorely driven, seeing that in truth I do not love her? I would not have her now for all the world. I know well how providential has been my escape. And yet I go about like a wounded animal, who can find none to consort with him. Till I met you, and learned to talk to you, I was truly miserable. And why? Because I had been saved from falling when standing on a precipice! Because the engine had not been allowed to crush me when passing along on its iron road! Ought I not to rejoice and be thankful rather, as I think of what I have escaped? But in truth it is the poor weakness of human nature. People say that I have been — jilted. What matters it to me what people say? I have been saved, and as time goes on I shall know it and be thankful.'

Every word of it came home to her and gave her back her own story. There was her own soreness, and her own salvation. There was the remembrance of what the people in Exeter were saying of her, only slightly relieved by the conviction that she had been preserved from a life of unhappiness. But she had never been able to look at it quite as he did. He knew that the better thing had happened to him; but she, though she knew it also, was sore at heart because people told the story, as she thought, to her discredit. There was, indeed, this difference between them. It was said truly of him, that the girl had jilted him, but falsely of her that she had been jilted.

She, however, told him nothing of her own life. There had come moments in which she was sorely tempted. But she had allowed them to pass by, telling herself on each occasion that this at any rate was not the moment. She could not do it now, — or now, — or now, lest there should seem to be some peculiar motive on her own part. And so the matter went on till there had arisen a feeling of free confidence on the one side, and of absolute restraint on the other. She could not do it, she said to herself. Much as she trusted Mr Western, deeply as she regarded him as her friend, strongly as she wished that the story had been told to him at some former passage of their intimacy, the proper time had

passed by, she said, and he must be left in his ignorance.

Then one day there happened that which the
outside world at Rome had long expected; and
among the number Mrs Holt. George Western
proposed to marry Cecilia Holt. Of all the world
at Rome who had watched the two together she
probably was the last who thought of any such
idea. But even to her the idea must surely have
come in some shape before the proposal. He had
allowed her to feel that he was only happy in her
company, and he had gradually fallen into the
habit of confiding to her in everything. He had
told her of his money, and of his future life. He
had consulted her about his books, and pictures
he had bought, and even about the servants of
his establishment. She cannot but have expected
it. But yet when the moment came she was
unable to give him an answer.

It was not that she did not think that she liked
him. She had been surprised to find how fond
she had gradually become of him; — how Sir
Francis had faded in her memory, and had
become a poor washed-out daub of a man while
this other had grown into the proportions of a
hero. She did not declare to herself that she
loved him, but she was sure that she could do so.
But two reasons did for a while make her feel
that she could not accept him. The one was weak
as water, but still it operated with her. Since she
had been abroad she had corresponded regularly
with Miss Altifiorla, and Miss Altifiorla in her

letters had been very strong in her aversion to matrimony. Many things had been said apparently with the intention of comforting Cecilia, but written in truth with the view of defending herself. 'I have chosen the better side, and have been true to it without danger of stumbling.' So it was that Miss Altifiorla put it. 'You, dearest Cecilia, have had an accident, but have recovered and stand once more upon the solid ground. Take care, oh take care, that you do not fall.' Cecilia did not remember that any chance of stumbling had come in Miss Altifiorla's way; and was upon the whole disgusted by the constancy of her friend's arguments. But still they did weigh, and drove her to ask herself whether, in truth, an unmarried life was not the safer for a woman. But the cause which operated the strongest with her was the silence which she had herself maintained. There was indeed no reason why she should not at once begin and tell her story. But in doing so it would appear that she had been induced to do it only by Mr Western's offer. And she cheated herself by some vague idea that she would be telling the secrets of another person. 'Had it been for myself only,' she said to herself, 'I would have done it long since. But that which made it improper then would make it still more improper now.' And so she held her peace and told Mr Western nothing of the story.

He came to her the day after his offer and demanded her answer. But she was not as yet able to give it to him. She had in the meantime told her mother, and had received from her that ready, willing, quick assurance of her sanction which was sure to operate in a different way than that intended. Her mother was thinking only of her material interests, — of a comfortable house and a steady, well-to-do life's companion. Of what more should she have thought? the reader will say. But Cecilia had still in her head undefined, vague notions of something which might be better than that, — of some companion who might be better than the companions which other girls generally choose for themselves. She dreamed of some one who should sit with her during the long mornings and read Dante to her, — when she should have taught herself to understand it; of some one with a hidden nobility of character which should be all but divine. Her invectives against matrimony had all come from a fear lest the man with the hidden nobility should not be forthcoming. She tried, or had nearly tried, Sir Francis Geraldine, and had made one hideous mistake. Was or was not this Mr Western a man with all such hidden nobility? If so she thought that she might love him.

She required a week, and gave her whole thoughts to the object. Should she or should she not abandon that mode of life to which she had certainly pledged herself? In the first days of the misery created by the Geraldine disruption she had declared that she would never more open her ears or her heart to matrimonial projects.

The promise had only been made to Miss Altifiorla, — to Miss Altifiorla and to herself. At the present moment she did not greatly regard Miss Altifiorla; — but the promise made to herself and corroborated by her assurance to another, almost overcame her. And then there was that story which she could not now tell to Mr Western. She could not say to him; — 'Yes, I will accept you, but you must first hear my tale'; and then tell him the exact copy of his own to her. And yet it was necessary that he should know. The time must come, — some day. Alas; she did not remember that no day could be less painful, — less disagreeable than the present. If he did not like the story now he could tell her so, and have done with it. There could be no fault found with her. It had hitherto been free to her to tell it or not as she pleased. 'I had not meant to have disclosed my secret, but now it is necessary.' Even had he fancied that she had 'invented it' in part and made it like to his own, no harm, — no dangerous harm would come from that. He could but be angry and recede from his offer. But she found that she did not wish him to recede. Her objections to matrimony had all been cured. She told herself at the last moment that she was not able to undergo the absurdity of such a revelation, — and she accepted him.

Chapter V

CECILIA'S
SECOND CHANCE

It became at once necessary that Mr Western should start off for London. That had been already explained. He would go, whether accepted or refused. When she had named a week, he had told her that he should only have just time to wait for her reply. She offered to be ready in five days, but he would not hurry her. During the week she had hardly seen him, but she was aware that he remained silent, moody, almost sullen. She was somewhat afraid of his temper; — but yet she had found him in other respects so open, so noble, so consistent! 'It shall be so,' she said, putting her hand into his. Then his very nature seemed to have changed. It appeared as though nothing could restrain him in the expression of his satisfaction. Nothing could be more quietly joyous than his manner. He was to have left Rome by a mid-day train, but he would wait for a train at midnight in order that he might once dine with his own wife that was to be. 'You will kill yourself with the fatigue,' Cecilia said. But he laughed at her. It was not so easy to kill him. Then he sat with her through the long morning, telling her of the doings of his past life, and his schemes for the life to come. He had a great book which he wanted to write, — as to which everybody might laugh at him but she must not laugh. And he laughed at himself and his aspiration; but she promised all her sympathy, and she told him of their house at Exeter, and of her mother's future loneliness. He would do anything for her within his power. Her mother should live with them if she wished it. And she spoke of the money which was to be her own, and told him of the offer which her mother had made as to giving up a portion of it. Of this he would have none. And he told her how it must be settled. And he behaved just as a lover should do, — taking upon himself to give directions, but giving all the directions just such as she would have them.

Then he went; and there came upon her a cold, chilling feeling that she had already been untrue to him. It was a feeling as to which she could not speak, even to her mother. But why had not her mother advised her and urged her to tell him everything? Her mother had said not a word to her about it. Why did her mother treat her as though she were one to be feared, and beyond the possibility of advice? But to her mother she said not a word on the subject. From the moment in which Mr Western had first begun to pay her attention, the name of Sir Francis had never been mentioned between the mother and daughter. And now in all their intercourse Mrs Holt spoke with an unclouded serenity of their future life. It was to her as though the Geraldine episode had been absolutely obliterated from the memory of them all. Mr Western to her was everything. She would not accept his magnificent offer of a home, because she knew that an old woman in a man's house could only be considered as in his way. She would divide her income, and give at any rate a third to her daughter. And she did bestow much advice as to the manner in which everything should be done so as to tend to his happiness. His tastes should be adopted, and his ways of life should be studied. His pursuits should be made her pursuits, and his friends her friends. All this was very well. Cecilia knew all that without any teaching from her mother. Her instincts told her as much as that. But what was she to do with this secret which loaded her bosom, but as to which she could not bring herself even to ask her mother's advice?

Then she made up her mind that she would write to her lover and relate the whole story as to Sir Francis Geraldine. And she did write it; but she was alarmed at finding that the story, when told, extended itself over various sheets of paper. And the story would take the shape of a confession, — as though she were telling her lover of some passage in her life of which she had cause to be ashamed. She knew that there was no ground for shame. She had done nothing which she ought not to have done, nothing which she could not have acknowledged to him without a blush. When the letter was completed, she found it to be one which she could not send. It was as though she were telling him something, on reading which he would have to decide whether their engagement should or should not be continued. This was not at all her purpose. Thinking of it all with a view to his happiness, and to his honour, she did not wish him to suppose that there could be a doubt on that subject. It was clear to her that a letter so worded was not fit for the occasion, and she destroyed it. Still she was minded to write to him, but for the moment she postponed her purpose. Of course she wrote to her friends in Exeter. Were she to be silent to them it would appear as though she were ashamed of what she was now doing. She told Maude Hippesley, — or Mrs Thorne as she was now called; and she told Mrs Green, and also Miss Altifiorla. Immediate answers came from the three. Those from the two married ladies were in all respects satisfactory. That from Mrs Thorne was quite enthusiastic in its praises of matrimony. That from Mrs Green was a little less warm, but was still discreetly happy. She had no doubt in her own mind that a married life was preferable, and that Mr Western, though perhaps a little old, was upon the whole a well-chosen and deserving consort for life. But the letter from Miss Altifiorla was very different from these, and as it had some effect perhaps in producing the circumstances which are to be told, it shall be given at length; —

'MY DEAR CECILIA, — I am of course expected to congratulate you, and as far as Mr

Western's merits are concerned, I do so with all my full heart. He is possessed, I have no doubt, of all those virtues which should adorn a husband, and is in all respects the very opposite to Sir Francis Geraldine. You give me to understand that he is steady, hard-working, and properly ambitious. In spite of the mistake which you made in reference to Sir Francis Geraldine, I will not doubt but that your judgment in respect to Mr Western will be found correct. If it is to be I dare say it could not be better. But must it be?' 'Of course it must,' said Cecilia to herself, feeling very angry with Miss Altifiorla for raising the question at such a time and in such a manner. 'After all the sweet converse and sweeter resolutions that have passed between us on this matter, must all be abandoned like a breath of summer wind, meaning nothing?' Of what infinitely bad taste was not the woman guilty, in thus raising the question when the only final answer to it had been already given? Cecilia felt ashamed of herself as she thought of this, in that she had admitted the friendship of such a friend. 'A breath of summer wind!' she said, repeating with scorn her friend's somewhat high-flown words. 'I cannot but say that, like Martha, you have chosen the worser part,' continued the letter. 'The things of the world, which are in themselves but accidents, have been for a moment all in all to you; but knowing you as I do, I am aware how soon they will fade away, and have no more than their proper weight. Then you will wake some day, and feel that you have devoted yourself to the mending of his stockings and the feeding of his babies.' There was something in this which stirred Cecilia to absolute wrath. If there were babies would they not be her babies as well as his? Was it not the intention of the Lord that the world should be populated? The worser part, indeed! Then she took up the cudgels in her own mind on behalf of Martha, as she had often done before. How would the world get on unless there were Marthas? And was it not more than probable that a self-dubbed Mary should fall into idle ways under the pretence that she was filled with special inspiration? Looking at Miss Altifiorla as a Mary, she was somewhat in love with the Marthas.

'I do not doubt that Mr Western is what he should be,' the letter went on, 'but even judging him by your letter, I find that he is autocratic and self-opinioned. It is his future life, and not yours, of which he is thinking, his success and not yours, his doings and not your doings.' 'How does she know?' exclaimed Cecilia. 'She has only my account of him, and not his of me.' 'And he is right in this,' went on the letter, 'because the ways of the world allow such privileges to men. What would a man be unless he took the place which his personal strength has obtained for him? For women, in the general, of course matrimony is fit. They have to earn their bread, and think of little else. To be a man's toy and then his slave, with due allowance for food and clothes, suffices for them. But I had dreamed a dream that it would not suffice for you. Alas, alas! I stand alone now in the expression of my creed. You must excuse me if I repine, when I find myself so cruelly deserted.'

All this Cecilia felt to be as absurd as it was ill-timed, — and to be redeemed, as it were, from its ill-nature by its ridiculous philosophy. But at last there came a paragraph which admitted of no such excuse. 'What has Mr Western said as to the story of Sir Francis Geraldine? Of course you have told him the whole, and I presume that he has pardoned that episode. In spite of the expression of feelings which I have been unable to control, you must believe, dear Cecilia, that I am as anxious as ever for your happiness, and am,

'Your most affectionate friend,
'FRANCESCA ALTIFIORLA.'

Cecilia, when she had completed the reading of the letter, believed nothing of the kind. That last paragraph about Sir Francis had turned all her kindly feelings into wrath, and contained one word which she knew not how to endure. She was told that Mr Western had 'pardoned' the Geraldine episode in her life. She had done nothing for which pardon had been necessary.

To merit pardon there must have been misconduct; and, as this woman had known all her behaviour in that matter, what right had she to talk of pardon? In what had she deserved pardon; — or at any rate the pardon of Mr Western? There had been a foolish engagement made between her and Sir Francis Geraldine, which had been most wisely dissolved. The sin, if sin there had been, was against Sir Francis, and certainly had never been considered as sin by this woman who now wrote to her. Was it a sin that she had loved before, a matter as to which Mr Western was necessarily in ignorance when he first came to her? But might it not come to pass that his pardon should be required in that the story had never been told to him? It was the sting which came from that feeling which added fierceness to her wrath. 'Of course you have told him the whole, and I presume that he has pardoned that episode!' She had not told Mr Western the whole, and had thus created another episode for which his pardon might be required. It was this that the woman had intended to insinuate, understanding with her little sharpness, with her poor appreciation of character, how probable it was that Cecilia should not have told him of her previous engagement.

She sat thinking of it all that night till the matter assumed new difficulties in her mind's eyesight. And she began to question to herself whether Mr Western had a right to her secret, — whether the secret did not belong to two persons, and she was bound to keep it for the sake of the other person. She had committed a wrong, an injury, or at any rate had inflicted a deserved punishment upon Sir Francis; one as to which a man would naturally much dislike that it should be noised about the world. Was she not bound to keep her secret still a secret for his sake? She was angry with herself when she asked the question, but still she asked it. She knew that she owed nothing to Sir Francis Geraldine, and that she owed all to Mr Western. But still she asked it, because in that way could she best strengthen herself against the telling of the story. The more she turned the matter in her mind, the more impossible to her became the task of telling it. At last she resolved that she would not tell it now. She would not tell it at any rate till she again saw him, — because Miss Altifiorla had told her that she 'presumed he had pardoned her that episode'.

It was arranged that they should be married at Exeter in April. Their house there was not yet vacant, but would be lent to them for a fortnight. After the marriage Mrs Holt would go into lodgings, and remain there till the house should be ready for her. But they were both to return to Exeter together, and then there would be bustle and confusion till the happy ceremony should have been performed. It was arranged that she should have but two bridesmaids, but she was determined that she would not ask Miss Altifiorla to be one of them. A younger sister of

Mrs Green and a younger sister also of Maude Hippesley were chosen. Miss Altifiorla, when she came to see Cecilia on her return, expressed herself as quite satisfied. 'It is best so, dear,' she said. 'I was afraid that you would ask me. Of course I should have done it, but my heart would not have been there. You can understand it all, I know.' Cecilia's wrath had become mitigated by this time, and she answered her friend civilly. 'Just so. You think I ought to be an old maid, and therefore do not like to lend a hand at turning me into a young wife. I have got two girls who have no objection on that score.' 'You might find a hundred in Exeter,' said Miss Altifiorla proudly, 'and yet I may be right in my opinions.'

Mr Western was to come down to Exeter only on the day before the marriage. The Holts had seen him as they came through London, where they slept one night, but as yet the story had not been told. Cecilia expected, almost wished, that the story might reach him from other quarters. It was so natural now that he should talk about the girl whom he intended to marry, and so natural, — as Cecilia thought, — that in doing so he should hear the name of Sir Francis Geraldine. Sir Francis was a man well known to the world of fashion, and many men must have heard of his intended marriage. Cecilia, though she almost hoped, almost feared that it should be so. The figure of Mr Western asking with an angry voice why he had not been told did alarm her. But he asked no such question, nor, as far as Cecilia knew, had he heard anything of Sir Francis when the Holts passed through London.

Nor did he seem to have heard it when he came down to Exeter. At any rate he did not say a word respecting Sir Francis. He spent the last evening with the Holts in their own house, and Cecilia felt that he had never before made himself so happy with her, so pleasant, and so joyous. It had been the same during their long walk together in the afternoon. He was so full of affairs which were his own, which were so soon to become her own, that there was not a moment for her in which she could tell the story. There are stories for the telling of which a peculiar atmosphere is required, and this was one of them. She could not interrupt him in the middle of his discourse and say: — 'Oh, by-the-bye, — there is something that I have got to say to you.' To tell the story she must tune her mind to the purpose. She must begin it in a proper tone, and be sure that he would be ready to hearken to it as it should be heard. She felt that the telling would be specially difficult in that it had been put off so long. But though she had made up her mind to tell it before she had started on her walk, the desirable moment never came. So she again put it off, saying that it should be done late at night when her mother had gone to her bed. The time came when he was alone with her, sitting with his arm around her waist, telling her of all the things she should do for him to make his life blessed; — and how he too would endeavour to do some little things for her in order that her life might be happy. She would not tell it then. Though little might come of it, she could not do it. And yet from day to day the feeling had grown upon her that it was certainly her duty to let him know that one accident in her life. There was no disgrace in it, no cause for anger on his part, nor even for displeasure if it had only been told him at Rome. He could then have taken her, or left her as he pleased. Of course he would have taken her, and the only trouble of her life would have been spared her. What possible reason could there have been that he should not take her? It was not any reason of that kind which had kept her silent. Of that she was quite confident. Indeed now she could not explain to herself why she had held her peace. It seemed to her as though she must have been mad to have let day after day go by at Rome and never to have mentioned to him the name of Sir Francis Geraldine. But such, alas, had been the fact. And now the time had come in which she found it to be impossible to tell the story. As she went for the last time to her solitary bed she endeavoured to console herself by thinking that he must have heard of it from other quarters. But then again she declared that he in his nobility would certainly not have been silent. He would have questioned her and then have told her that all was right between them. But now as she tossed unhappily on her pillow she told herself that all was wrong.

Chapter VI

WHAT ALL HER FRIENDS SAID ABOUT IT

And 'all went merry as a marriage bell'. George Western and Cecilia Holt were married in the Cathedral by the Dean, who was thus supposed to show his great anger at his brother-in-law's conduct. And this was more strongly evinced by the presence of all the Hippesleys; — for all were there to grace the ceremony except Maude, who was still absent with her young squire, and who wrote a letter full of the warmest affection and congratulations, which Cecilia received on that very morning. Miss Altifiorla also came to the Cathedral, with pink bows in her bonnet, determined to show that though she were left alone in her theory of life she did not resent the desertion. And Mrs Green was there, humble and sweet-tempered as ever, snubbing her husband a little who assisted at the altar, and whispering a word into her friend's ears to assure her that she had done the proper thing.

It is hardly necessary to say that on the morning of her wedding it was in truth impossible for Cecilia to tell the story. It had now to be left untold with what hope there might be for smoothing it over in some future stage of her married life. She had done the deed now, and had married the man with the untold secret in

68

her heart. The sin surely could not be of a nature to weigh so deeply on her conscience! She endeavoured to comfort herself with that idea again and again. How many girls are married who have been engaged to, or at least in love with, half-a-dozen suitors before the man has come who is at last to be their lord! But Cecilia told herself, as she endeavoured thus to find comfort, that her nature was not such as theirs. This thing which she had done was a sin or not a sin, according as it might be regarded by the person who did it. It was a sin to her, a heavy grievous sin, and one that weighed terribly on her conscience as she repeated the words after the Dean at the altar that morning. There was a moment in which she almost refused to repeat them, — in which she almost brought herself to demand that she might retire for a time with him who was not yet her husband, and give him another chance. Her mind entertained an exaggerated feeling of it, a feeling which she felt to be exaggerated but which she could not restrain. In the meantime the service went on; the irrevocable word was spoken; and when it was done she was led away into the cathedral vestry as sad a bride as might be.

And yet nobody had seen her trouble. With a capacity for struggling, infinitely greater than that possessed by any man, she had smiled and looked happy beneath her bridal finery, as though no grief had weighed heavily at her heart. And he was as jocund a bridegroom as ever put a ring upon a lady's finger. All that gloom of his, which had seemed to be his nature till after she had accepted him, had vanished altogether. And he carried himself with no sheepish, shamefaced demeanour as though half ashamed of the thing which he had done. He seemed as proud to be a bridegroom as ever girl was to become a bride. And in truth he was proud of her and did think that he had chosen well. After the former troubles of his life he did feel that he had brought himself to a happy haven at last.

There was a modest breakfast at Mrs Holt's house, from which the guests departed quickly as soon as the bride and bridegroom had been taken away to the railway station. But when the others were gone Miss Altifiorla remained, — out of kindness. Mrs Holt need make no stranger of her, and it would be so desolate for her to be alone. So surmised Miss Altifiorla. 'I suppose,' said she, when she had fastened up the pink ribbons so that they might not be soiled by the trifle with which she prepared to regale herself while she asked the question, 'I suppose that he knows all the story about that other man?'

'Why should he?' asked Mrs Holt in a sharp tone that was quite uncommon to her.

'Well; I do not know much about such things, but I presume it is common to tell a gentleman when anything of that kind has occurred.'

'What business has he to know? And what can it matter? Perhaps he does know it.'

'But Cecilia has not told him?'

70

'Why should she tell him? I don't think that it is a thing we need talk about. You may be quite sure that Cecilia has done what is proper.' In saying this Mrs Holt belied her own thoughts. Cecilia had never said a word to her about it, nor had she dared to say a word to her own daughter on the subject. She had been intently anxious that her daughter should be married, and when she had seen Mr Western in the act of falling in love, had studiously abstained from all subjects which might bring about a reference to Sir Francis Geraldine. But she had felt that her daughter would make that all straight. Her daughter was so much more wise, so much more certain to do what was right, so much more high-minded than was she, that she considered herself bound to leave all that to Cecilia. But as the days went on and the hour fixed for the marriage became nearer and nearer she had become anxious. Something seemed to tell her that a duty had been omitted. But the moment had never come in which she had been able to ask her daughter. And now she would not endure to be cross-examined on the subject by Miss Altifiorla.

But Miss Altifiorla was not at all afraid of Mrs Holt and was determined to push the question a little further. 'He ought to know, you know. I am sure Cecilia will have thought that.'

'If he ought to know then he does know,' said Mrs Holt with great certainty. 'I am sure we may leave all that to Cecilia herself. If he is satisfied with her, it does not matter much who else may be dissatisfied.'

'Oh, if he is satisfied, that is enough,' said Miss Altifiorla as she took her leave. But she felt sure that the secret had not been told and that it ought to have been told, and she felt proud to think that she had spotted the fault. Cecilia Holt would have done very well in the world had she confined herself, — as she had solemnly promised, — to those high but solitary feminine duties to which Miss Altifiorla had devoted herself. But she had chosen to make herself the slave of a man who, — as Miss Altifiorla expressed it to herself, — 'would turn upon her and rend her'. And she, Miss Altifiorla, had seen and did see it all. The time might come when the wounded dove would return to her care. Of course she hoped that the time would not come; — but it might.

'I'll tell you one thing,' said Mrs Green to her husband as they walked home from the breakfast. 'That girl has not yet said a word to that man about Sir Francis Geraldine.'

'What makes you think that, my dear?'

'Think it! I know it. It was not likely that there should be much talk about Sir Francis either in the Cathedral or at the breakfast; but one can tell from other things whether a subject has been avoided. These are plain when little things would have been said but are not said. There has been no allusion made to their reason for leaving the house.'

'I don't see that it signifies much, my dear.'

'Oh, doesn't it? What would you have thought if after I had become engaged to you you had found that a month or two before I had been engaged to another man?'

'It is more than twelve months, my dear.'

'No, it is not more than twelve months since first they met in Italy. I know what I am talking about and you need not contradict me. You'll find that he'll learn it of a sudden, and then all the fat will be in the fire. I know what men are.' It was thus that the gentle Mrs Green expressed herself on the subject to her husband.

At the Deanery the matter was spoken of in a different tone but still with similar feelings. 'I don't think Cecilia has ever yet said a word to that poor man as to her engagement with Francis. I cannot tell what has put it into my mind, but I think that it is so.' It was thus that Mrs Hippesley spoke to the Dean.

'Your brother behaved very badly; — very badly,' said the Dean.

'That has got nothing to do with it. Mr Western won't care a straw whether Francis behaved well or ill. And for the matter of that I don't think that as yet we quite know the truth of it. Nor would he care if his wife had behaved ill to the other man, so long as she behaved well to him. But if he has heard nothing of it and now finds it out he's not the man I take him to be if he don't let her hear of it.'

'It's nothing to us,' said the Dean.

'Oh, no; it's nothing to us. But you'll see that

what I say comes true.' In this way all the world of Cecilia's friends were talking on the matter which she had mentioned to no one. She still hoped that her husband might have heard the story, and that he kept it buried in his bosom. But it never occurred to her that it would become matter of discussion among her friends at Exeter.

There was one other person who also discussed it very much at his ease. Sir Francis Geraldine among his friends in London had been congratulated on his safe but miraculous escape. With a certain number of men he had been wont to discuss the chances of matrimony. Should he die, without having an heir, his title and property would go to his cousin, Captain Geraldine, who was a man some fifteen years younger than himself and already in possession of a large fortune. There were many people in the world whom Sir Francis hated, but none whom he hated so cordially as his cousin. Three or four years since he had been ill, nearly to dying, and had declared that he never would have recovered but for the necessity that he was under to keep his cousin out of the baronetage. It had therefore become imperative on him to marry in order that there might be an heir to the property. And though he had for a few weeks been perfectly contented with his Cecilia, there could be no doubt that he had experienced keenly the sense of relief when she had told him that the engagement must be at an end. Another marriage must be arranged, but there would be time for that; and he would take care, that on this occasion he would not put himself into the hands of one who was exigeante and had a will of her own. 'By Jove,' he said to his particular friend, Dick Ross, 'I would almost sooner that my cousin Walter had the property than put it and myself into the hands of such a virago.'

'You'll only get another,' said Dick, 'that will not let on, but will turn out to be twice as bad in the washing.'

'That I hardly think probable. There are many things which go to the choice of a wife, and the worst of it is that they are not compatible one with another. A woman should be handsome; but then she is proud. A woman should have a certain air of dignity; but when she has got it she knows that herself, and shows it off in the wrong place. She should be young; but if she is too young she is silly; wait a little and she becomes strong-minded and headstrong. If she don't read anything she becomes an ass and a bore; but if she do she despises a man because he is not always doing the same thing. If she is a nobody the world thinks nothing of her. If she come of high birth she thinks a deal too much of herself. It is difficult.'

'I'd have nothing to do with any of them,' said Dick Ross.

'And let that puppy come in! He wrote to me to congratulate me on my marriage, just when he knew it was off.'

75

'I'll tell you what I'd do,' said Dick. 'I'd marry some milk-maid and keep her down on the property. I'd see that it was all done legally and I'd take the kid away when he was three or four years old.'

'Everybody would talk about it.'

'Let 'em talk,' said Dick heroically. 'They couldn't talk you out of your ease or your pleasure or your money. I never could find out the harm of people talking about you. They might say whatever they pleased of me for five hundred a year.'

Then there came the news that Cecilia Holt was going to marry Mr Western. The tidings reached Sir Francis while the lovers were still at Rome. Of Mr Western Sir Francis knew something. In the first place his cousin Walter Geraldine had taken away the girl to whom Mr Western had in the first instance been engaged. And then they were in some degree neighbours, each possessing a small property in Berkshire. Sir Francis had bought his now some years since for racing purposes. It was adjacent to Ascot, and had been let or used by himself during the racing week, as he had or had not been short of money. Mr Western's small property had come to him from his uncle. But he had held it always in his own hands, and intended now to take his bride there as soon as their short honeymoon trip should be over. In this way Sir Francis had come to know something of Cecilia's husband, and did not especially love him. 'That young lady of mine has picked up old Western on her travels.' This Sir Francis said to his friend Ross up in London. The reader however must remember that 'old Western' was in fact a younger man than Sir Francis himself.

'I suppose he's welcome to her?' said Ross.

'I'm not so sure of that. Of course he is welcome in one way. She'll make him miserable and he'll do as much for her. You may let them alone for that.'

'Why should you care about it?'

'Well; I don't know. A fellow has a sort of feeling about a girl when he has been spooning on her himself. He doesn't want to think that another fellow is to pick her up immediately.'

'Dog in the manger, you mean.'

'You may call it that if you like. You never cared for any young woman, I suppose?'

'Oh, haven't I? Lots of 'em. But if I couldn't get a girl myself I never cared who had her. What's the good of being selfish?'

'What's the good of lying?' said Sir Francis, propounding a great doctrine in sociology. 'If I feel cut up what's the use of saying I don't, — unless I want to deceive the man I'm talking to? If I feel that I'd like a girl to be punished for her impertinence what's the use of my pretending to myself that I don't want it? If I wish a person to be injured, what's the use of saying I wish them all the good in the world, — unless there's something to be gained by my saying it? Now I don't care to tell you lies. I am quite willing that you should know all the truth about me. Therefore I tell you that I'm not best pleased that this minx should have already picked up another man.'

'He has the devil of a temper,' said Dick Ross, wishing to make the matter as pleasant as possible to his friend.

'So your Miss Holt is married,' Ross said to his friend on the day after the ceremony.

'Yes; she is married, and her troubles have now to begin. I wonder whether she has told him the little episode of our loves.'

'You may be sure of that,' said Dick.

'I am not at all so sure of it. She may have told him when they first became acquainted, but I cannot imagine her telling him afterwards. He is as proud as she, and is just the man not to like it.'

'It doesn't much signify to you, at any rate,' said the indifferent Dick.

'I'm not so sure of that,' said Sir Francis. 'I like the truth to be told. It may become my duty to take care that poor Mr Western shall know all about it.'

'What a beast that fellow is for mischief!' said Dick Ross as he walked home from his club that evening.

Chapter VII

MISS ALTIFIORLA'S ARRIVAL

Yes; — Sir Francis Geraldine was a beast for mischief! Thinking the matter over he resolved that Mr Western should not be left in the dark as to his wife's episode. And he determined that Mr Western would think more of the matter if it were represented to him that his wife had been jilted, and had been jilted unmistakably before they two had met each other on the Continent. He was right in this. According to the usages of the world the lady would have less to say for herself if that were the case and would have more difficulty in saying it. Therefore the husband would be the more bound to hear it. Sir Francis was a beast for mischief, but he knew what he was about.

But so did not Mrs Western when she allowed those opportunities to pass by her which came to her for telling her story before her marriage. In very truth she had had no reason for concealing it but that his story had been so nearly the same. On this account she had put it off, and put it off; — and then the fitting time had passed by. When she was with him alone after their marriage she could not do it, — without confessing her fault in that she had not done it before. She could not bring herself to do so. Standing so high in his esteem as she did and conscious that he was

79

thoroughly happy in his appreciation of her feminine merit, she could not make him miserable by descending from her pedestal to the telling of a story, which was disgraceful in that it had not been told before.

And there was a peculiarity of manner in him of which she became day by day more conscious. He could be very generous for good conduct to those dependent on him, but seemed to be one who could with difficulty forgive an injury. He wished to have everything about him perfect, and then life should go as soft as a summer's day. He was almost idolatrous to her in these first days of their marriage, but then he had found nothing out. Cecilia knowing his character asked herself after all what there was to be found out. How often that question must occur to the girl just married! But there was nothing. He was pleased with her person; pleased with her wit; pleased that money should have been offered to him, and pleased that for the present he should have declined it. He liked her dress and her willingness to change any portion of it at his slightest hint. He liked her activity and power of walking and her general adaptability to himself. He was pleased with everything. But she had the secret at her heart.

'I wonder that you should have lived so long, and never have been in love before,' he said to her one day as they were coming home.

'How do you know?' She blushed as she answered him, but it was a matter as to which

80

any girl might blush.

'I am sure you were not. I should have heard it.' And yet she was silent. She felt at the moment that the time had come, — the only possible time. But she let the moment pass by. Though she was ever thinking of her secret, and ever wishing that she could tell it, longing that it had been told, she could not bear that it should be surprised from her in this way. 'I think it nicer as it is,' he added as he left the room.

Then she got up and stood alone on the floor, thinking of it all. There she stood for ten minutes thinking of it. She would follow him and, not throwing herself on her knees — but standing boldly before him, tell him all. There was no disgrace in it, — to have loved that other man. Of her own conduct she was confident before all the world. There had been so little secrecy about it that she almost had a right to suppose that it had been known to all men. The more she tried to bring herself to follow him and tell him, the more she assured herself that there should be no necessity. How ought she to have told him, and when? At every point of his story should she have made known to him the same point in hers? 'It was exactly the same with me.' 'I wouldn't have my young man because he was indifferent.' 'With yours there was another lover ready. That has yet to come with me.' 'You have come abroad for consolation. So have I.' It would have been impossible; — was impossible. 'I think it nicer as it is,' he had said, and she could not do it.

There was some security while they were travelling, and she wished that they might travel for ever. She was happy while with him alone; — and so too was he. But for her secret she was completely happy. Let him only be kept in the dark and he would be happy always. She idolised him as her own. She loved him the better for thinking that 'it was nicer as it is'; — or would have done, had it been so. Why should they go where some sudden tidings might mar his joy; — where some sudden tidings certainly would do so sooner or later? Still they went on and on till in May they reached their house in Berkshire, — he with infinite joy at his heart, and she with the load upon hers.

Early in May they reached Durton Lodge, in Berkshire, and there they stayed during the summer. Mr Western had his house in London, and there was a question whether they would not go there for the season. But Cecilia had begged to be taken to her house in the country, and there she remained. Durton Lodge was little more than a cottage, but it was very pretty and prettily situated. When the Ascot week came he offered to take her there, but offered it with a smile which she understood to mean that his proposal should not be accepted. Indeed she had no wish for Ascot or for any place in which he or she must meet their old friends. Might it not be possible if they both could be happy at Durton that there they might remain with some minimum of intercourse with the world? Six months had now passed by since they had become engaged and no good-natured friend had as yet told him the truth. Might it not be possible that the same silence should be yet preserved? If years could be made to run on, then he would have become used to her and the telling of the secret would not be so severe.

But there came to her a great trouble in regard to her letters from Exeter. Miss Altifiorla would fill hers with long statements about Sir Francis which had no interest whatsoever, but which required to be at once destroyed. She soon learnt in her married life that her husband had no wish to see her letters. She would so willingly have shown them to him, would have taken such a joy in asking for his sympathy, such a delight in exposing Miss Altifiorla's peculiar views of life, that she lost much by her constrained reticence. But this necessity of destroying papers was very grievous to her. Though she knew that he would not read the letters without her permission still she must destroy them. In every possible way she endeavoured to silence her correspondent, not answering her at first, and then giving her such answers as were certainly not affectionate. But in no way would Miss Altifiorla 'be snubbed'. Then after a while she proposed to come and stay a week at Durton Lodge. This was not to be endured. The very thought of it filled poor Mrs Western's heart with despair. And yet she did not like to refuse without telling her husband. Of Miss Altifiorla she had already made mention, and Mr Western had been taught to laugh at the peculiarities of the old maid. 'Pray do not have her,' she said to him. 'She will make you very uncomfortable, and my life will be a burden to me.'

'But what can you say to her?'

'No room,' suggested Cecilia.

'But there are two rooms.'

'I know there are. But is one to be driven by a strict regard for literal truth to entertain an unwelcome friend? Miss Altifiorla thought that I ought not to have married you, and as I thought I ought we had some words about it.'

'Whom did she want you to marry?' asked Mr Western, with a laugh.

'Nobody. She is averse to marriage altogether.'

'Unless she was the advocate of some other suitor, I do not see that I need quarrel with her. But she is your friend and not mine, and if you choose to put her off of course you can do so. I would advise you to find something more probable than the want of a bedroom in a house in which one is only occupied.'

There was truth in this. What reason could she find? Knowing her husband's regard to truth she did not dare to suggest any reason to her friend more plausible than the want of a room, but still essentially false. She was driven about thinking that she would get her husband to take her away from home for awhile — for two or three days. The letter remained unanswered, when her husband suggested to her that she had better write.

'Could we not go somewhere?' she replied with a look of trouble on her brow.

'Run away from home on account of Miss Altifiorla?' said he. She was beginning to be afraid of him and knew that it was so. She did not dare to declare to him her thoughts and was afraid at every moment that he should read them.

'Then I must just tell her that we can't have her.'

'That will be best, — if you have made up your mind. As far as I am concerned she is welcome. Any friend of yours would be welcome.'

'Oh, George, she would bore you out of your life!'

'I am not so easily bored. I am sure that any intimate friend of yours would have something to say for herself.'

'Oh, plenty.'

'And as for her having been an advocate for single life, she had not seen me and therefore her reasons could not have been personal. There are a great many young women, thirty years old and upwards, who take up the idea. They do not wish to subject themselves, — perhaps because they have not been asked by the right person.'

'I don't think there have been any persons here. Not that she is bad-looking.'

'Perhaps you think I shall fall in love with her.'

'I'd have her directly. But she is the last person in the world I should think of.'

'I can get on very well with any one who has an

idea. There is at any rate something to strike at. The young lady who agrees with everything and suggests nothing, is to me the most intolerable. At any rate you had better make up your mind at once or you'll have her here before you know where you are.'

It was this which did, indeed, happen. On the day after the last conversation Mrs Western wrote her letter. In it she expressed her sorrow that engagements for the present prevented her from having the power to entertain her friend. No doubt the letter was cold and unfriendly. As she read it over to herself she declared that she would have been much hurt to have received such a letter from her friend. But she declared again that under no circumstances could she have offered herself as Miss Altifiorla had done. Nevertheless she felt ashamed of the letter. All of which, however, became quite unnecessary when, in the course of the afternoon, Miss Altifiorla appeared at Durton Lodge. She arrived with a torrent of reasons. She had come up to London on business which admitted of no excuse. She was sure that her friend's letter must have gone astray, — that letter which for the last three days she had been expecting. To return from London to Exeter without seeing her dear friend would be so unfeeling and unnatural! She must have come to Durton Lodge or must have returned to Exeter. In fact, she so put it as to make it appear impossible that she should not have come.

'My dear Miss Altifiorla,' said Mr Western, 'I am sure that Cecilia is delighted to see you. And as for me, you are quite welcome.' But, as a fact, there she was. There was no sending her away again; — no getting her out of the house without a sojourn of some days. Whatever mischief she might do might be done at once. There could be no doubt that she would begin to talk of Sir Francis Geraldine and declare the secret which it was now the one care of Cecilia's mind to keep away from her husband. It mattered not that her presence there showed her to be vulgar, impertinent, and obtrusive. There she was, and must be dealt with as a friend, — or as an enemy. Again Cecilia almost made up her mind as to the better course. Let her go to her husband and tell him all, and tell him also why it was that she told him now. Let her endure his anger, and then there would be an end of it. There was nothing else as to which she had need to dread him.

But again, when she found herself with him, he was happy, and jocund, and jested with her about her friend. She could not get him into the humour in which it was proper that he should be told. She did not tell him, and went down to dinner with the terrible load about her heart. Three or four times during the evening the conversation was on the point of turning to matters in which the name of Sir Francis Geraldine would surely be mentioned. With infinite care, but without showing her care, she contrived to master the subject, and to force her friend and her husband to talk of other things. But the struggle was very great, and she was aware that it could not be repeated. The reader will remember, perhaps, the stern thoughts which Miss Holt had entertained as to her friend when her friend had thought proper to give her some idea of what her duty ought to be in regard to her present husband. She remembered well that Miss Altifiorla had written to her, asking whether Mr Western had forgiven 'that episode'. And her mother, too, had in writing dropped some word, — some word intended to be only half intelligible as to the question which Miss Altifiorla had asked after the wedding breakfast. She knew well what had been in the woman's mind, and knew also what had been in her own! She remembered how proudly she had disdained the advice of this woman when it had been given to her. And yet now she must go to her and ask for mercy. She saw no other way out of her immediate trouble. She did not believe but that her friend would be silent when told to be silent; but yet how painfully disgraceful to her, the bride, would be the telling.

She went up to Miss Altifiorla's room after she had gone for the night, and found her friend getting into bed, happy with the assistance of a strange maid. 'Oh my dear,' said Miss Altifiorla, 'my hair is not half done yet; are you in a hurry for Mary?'

'I will go to my own room,' said Mrs Western, 'and when Mary will tell me that you are ready I will come to you. There is something I have to tell you.' She had not been five minutes in her own room before Mary summoned her. The 'something to be told' took immediate hold of Miss Altifiorla's imagination, and induced her to be ready for bed with her hair, we may suppose, half 'done'.

'Francesca,' said Mrs Western, as soon as she entered the room, 'I have a favour to ask you.'

'A favour?'

'Yes, a favour.' She had come prepared with her request down to the very words in which it should be uttered. 'I do not wish you, while you remain here, to make any allusion to Sir Francis Geraldine.' Miss Altifiorla almost whistled as she heard the words spoken. 'You understand me, do you not? I do not wish any word to be said which may by chance lead to the mention of Sir Francis Geraldine's name. If you will under-stand that, you will be able to comply with my wishes.' Her request she made almost in the stern words of an absolute order. There was nothing humble in her demeanour, nothing which seemed to tell of a suppliant. And having given her command she remained quiet, waiting for an answer.

'Then this was the reason why you didn't answer me. You did not want to see me, and therefore remained silent.'

'I did not want to see you. But it was not on that account that I remained silent. I should have written to you. Indeed I have written to you, and the letter would have gone today. I wrote to you putting you off. But as you are here I have to tell you my wishes. I am sure that you will do as I would have you.'

'I have to think of my duty,' said Miss Altifiorla.

Then there came a black frown on Mrs Western's brow. Duty! What duty could she have in such a matter, except to her? She suspected the woman of a desire to make mischief. She felt confident that the woman would do so unless repressed by the extraction from her of a promise to the contrary. She did believe that the woman would keep her word, — that she would feel herself bound to preserve herself from the accusation of direct falsehood; but from her good feeling, from her kindness, from her affection, from that feminine bond which ought to have made her silent, she expected nothing. 'Your duty, Francesca, in this matter is to me,' said Mrs Western, assuming a wonderful severity of manner. 'You have known me many years and are bound to me by many ties. I tell you what my wishes are. I cannot quite explain my reasons, but I do not doubt that you will guess them.'

'You have kept the secret?' said Miss Altifiorla with a devilish mixture of malice, fun, and cunning.

'It does not matter what I have done. There are reasons, which made me wish to avoid your immediate coming. At the present moment it would interfere gravely with his happiness and with mine were he to learn the circumstances of Sir Francis Geraldine's courtship. Of course it is painful to me to have to say this to you. It is so painful that to avoid it I have absolutely written to you telling you not to come. This I have done not to avoid your coming, which would otherwise have been a pleasure to me, but to save myself from this great pain. Now you know it all, and know also what it is that I expect from you.'

Miss Altifiorla listened to this in silence. She was seated in an easy bedroom chair, clothed from head to foot in a pale pink dressing-gown, from which the colour was nearly washed out; and her hair as I have said was 'half done'. But in her trouble to collect her thoughts she became quite unaware of all accessories. Her dear friend Cecilia had put the matter to her so strongly that she did not quite dare to refuse. But yet what a fund of gratification might there not be in telling such a story under such circumstances to the husband! She sat silent for a while meditating on it, till Mrs Western roughly forced a reply from her lips. 'I desire to have your promise,' said Mrs Western.

'Oh yes, of course.'

'You will carefully avoid all allusion to the subject.'

'Since you wish it, I will do so.'

'That is sufficient. And now good night.'

'I know that I am doing wrong,' said Miss Altifiorla.

'You would indeed be doing wrong,' said Mrs

Western, 'if you were to take upon yourself to destroy my happiness on such a matter after having been duly warned.'

Chapter VIII

LADY GRANT

It is literally true that the tongue will itch with a desire to tell a secret. Miss Altifiorla's tongue did itch. But upon the whole she endured her suffering, and kept her promise. She did not say a word in Mr Western's hearing which led to Sir Francis Geraldine as a topic of conversation. But in reward for this she exacted from Mrs Western an undertaking to keep her at Durton Lodge for a fortnight. The bargain was not exactly struck in those words, but it was so made that Mrs Western understood how great was the price she paid, and how valuable the article which she received in return. 'A fortnight!' Mr Western said, when his wife told him of the promise she had made. 'I thought that three days would have been too much for you.'

'Three hours are too much, — as interrupting our happiness. But as she is here, and as we have been very intimate for many years, and as she herself has named the time, I have not liked to contradict her.'

'So be it. She will interfere much more with you than with me, and I suppose that the coming will not be frequently repeated.'

Two days after this another guest proposed to visit them. But this was only for two nights, and her coming had in fact been expected from a period before the marriage. Lady Grant was Mr Western's younger sister, and the person of whom in all the world he seemed to think the most. Indeed he had assured his wife that next to herself she was the nearest and the dearest to him. She was a widow, and went but little into society. According to his account she was clever, agreeable and beautiful. She lived altogether in Scotland, where her time was devoted to her children, and was now coming up to England chiefly with the purpose of seeing her brother's wife. She was to be at Durton Lodge now only for a couple of nights, and then to return and remain with the understood purpose of taking them with her back to Scotland. Of Lady Grant Cecilia had become much afraid, as thinking it more than probable that her secret might be known to her. But it seemed that as yet Lady Grant knew nothing of it. She corresponded frequently with her brother, and as far as Cecilia could tell, the subject had not yet been mentioned between them. Could it be possible that all this time the secret was known to her husband and to her husband's sister? If so his silence to her was almost cruel.

Up to the morning of her coming Miss Altifiorla had certainly kept her promise. She had kept her promise, though there had been twenty little openings in which it would have been so easy for her to lead the way to the matter as to which her tongue longed to be speaking.

When any mention was made of Baronets either married or unmarried, of former lovers, of broken vows, or of second engagements, Miss Altifiorla would look with a meaning glance at her hostess. But of these glances Cecilia would apparently take no heed. She had soon got to know that Miss Altifiorla's promise would be kept unless she were led by some other person into an indirect breach of it. Cecilia's life during the period was one of great agony. But still she endured it without allowing her husband to perceive that it was so.

Now, on the coming of Lady Grant, what steps should she take? Should she ask her friend to be silent also to this second person, or should she presume the promise to be so extended? She could not bring herself to make a second request. The task of doing so was too ponderous. Miss Altifiorla's manner of receiving the request made it such a burden that she could not submit herself to it. The woman looked at her and spoke to her in a manner which she was obliged to endure without seeming to endure aught that was unnatural. She thought of her own struggles during that evening in the bedroom, and could see the woman as she sat struggling, in her pale pink dressing-gown, to escape from the necessity of promising. She could not have another such scene as that. But she thought that perhaps with one added word the promise might be made to suffice.

When they were alone together Miss Altifiorla

would constantly refer to the Geraldine affair. This was to be expected and to be endured. There would come an end to the fortnight and the woman would be gone. 'Do you think that Lady Grant knows?' she said, in the whisper that had become usual to her on such occasions.

'I am sure she knows nothing about it,' said Cecilia.

'How can you be sure? You do not know her and have never seen her. It will be very odd if she has not heard.'

'At any rate nothing need be said to her in this house. No hint need be made to her either by you or me.'

'I think she must have heard it. I happen to know that she has a great correspondence. Laws! when you think of who Sir Francis is and of the manner in which he lives, it is almost impossible to conceive that a person should not have heard of it.'

'We need not tell her.'

'You are quite safe with me. I have given you my word, and that ought to be enough. Nobody could have been more studious to avoid the matter; — though, indeed, it has sometimes been difficult. And then there has been my feeling of doubt whether my duty ought not to make me divulge it.' There was something in this which was peculiarly painful to Cecilia. The duty of this woman to her husband, to him whom she loved so truly, to him with whom it was in the very core of her heart to have everything in common! Francesca Altifiorla to speak of her duty to him! But even this had to be borne. 'Indeed, I feel every day that I am staying here that I am sacrificing duty to friendship.' Oh, into what trouble had she fallen without any sin of her own, — as she told herself; — without, at least, any great sin. When was the moment at which she ought to have told the story? She thought that she could remember the exact moment; when he had come back to her for her answer at the end of that week. And then she had not told him, simply from her dislike to repeat back to him the story which she had heard from himself!

Lady Grant came, and nothing could be sweeter or more gracious than the meeting. Miss Altifiorla was not there, and the two ladies, in the presence of the husband and brother, received each other with that quick intimacy and immediate loving friendship which it is given only to women to entertain. Lady Grant was ten years the senior and a widow, and had that air of living through the evening of her life instead of still enjoying the morning, which is peculiar to widows who have loved their husbands. She was very lovely, even in her mitigated widow's weeds, with a tall figure, and oval pale face, rather thin, but not meagre or attenuated. And Cecilia thought that she saw in her a determination to love her, and she on her side at once determined that she would return Lady Grant's affection. But not for that reason was her secret to be known. She looked on Lady Grant, as one whom she would so willingly have made her friend in all things, but still as one whom, as to that single matter, she could not but regard as her enemy.

They sat together for a couple of hours before dinner, and then at night there was another sitting from which Miss Altifiorla was again banished. And there were some joking questions asked and answers given as to Miss Altifiorla's presence. There was a something in the manner and gait of Lady Grant which made Cecilia almost ashamed of her Exeter friend. It was not that Miss Altifiorla was ignorant, or unladylike, or ill-dressed; but that she knew her friend too well. Miss Altifiorla was little and mean, whereas Cecilia was ready to accept her sister-in-law as great and noble. Miss Altifiorla was not therefore spoken of in the highest terms, and the mode of her coming to Durton Lodge without an invitation was subjected to some little ridicule.

But Mrs Western when she went to her room was comforted at any rate in thinking that Lady Grant did not know her secret. How poor must have been her state of comfort may be judged from the fact that this could add to it. On the following morning they met at breakfast, and all went well. But Lady Grant could not but notice that the young lady from Devonshire seemed to exercise an authority incommensurate with the tone in which she had been described. The day passed by happily enough, and Cecilia was strong in hope that Lady Grant might take her departure without a reference to her one subject of sorrow.

That night, however, her comfort, such as it was, was brought to an end. As they were sitting together in Lady Grant's bedroom Cecilia's ears were suddenly wounded by the mention of the name of Sir Francis Geraldine. In her immediate agony she could hardly tell how it occurred, but she was rapidly asked a question as to her former engagement. In the asking of it there was nothing rough, nothing unkind, nothing intended to wound, nothing to show a feeling that it should not be so; — but the question had been asked. There was the fact that Lady Grant knew the whole story.

But there was the fact also that her husband did not know it, or else that other fact which she would have given the world to know to be a fact, — that he knew it, and had willingly held his peace respecting it, even to his sister. If that could be so, then she would be happy; if that could be so, — if she could know that it was so, — then might she afford to despise Miss Altifiorla and her tyranny. But though the word had been not yet a moment uttered, she could not at first remember how it had been said. There was simply the knowledge that the name of Sir Francis Geraldine had been used, and that it had been declared that she had been engaged to him. Up to this moment she had been very grave, and very powerful, too, over herself. Up to this she had never betrayed herself. But now her courage gave way, the colour came to her cheeks and forehead and neck, and then passed rapidly away, — and she betrayed herself. 'Does not he know it?' asked Lady Grant. As she said the words she put out her hand and pressed Cecilia's in her own; and the tone of her voice was loving, and friendly, and sisterly. Though there was reproach in it, it was not half so bitter as that which Cecilia was constantly addressing to herself. The reproach was in her ears and not in Lady Grant's voice. But the words were repeated before Cecilia could answer them. 'Does not he know it?'

All her hope was thus abolished. Almost from the moment of Lady Grant's coming into the house she had taught herself to think that he must know it. It was impossible that the two should be ignorant, and impossible also, as she thought, that the sister should know it and that he should not. But all that was now at an end. It was necessary that she should answer her sister's question, and yet so difficult to find words in which to do so. She attempted to speak but the word would not come. Even the one word, 'No', would not form itself on her lips. She fell upon her knees and burying her face in Lady Grant's lap, thus told her secret.

'He has never heard of it?' again asked Lady Grant. 'Oh, my dear. That should not have been so; — must not be so.'

'If I could tell you! If I could tell you!'

'Tell me what? I am sure there is nothing for

you to tell which you need blush to speak.'

'No, no. Nothing, nothing.'

'Then why should he not know? Why should he not have known? Cecilia, you will tell him to-night before he goes to his rest?'

'No, — no. Not to-night. It is impossible. I must wait till that woman has gone.'

'Miss Altifiorla knows it?'

'Oh, yes.'

'She knows, too, that he does not know it?' This question Cecilia answered only by some sign. 'I fancied that it might be so. I thought that there was something between you which had been kept from him. Why, why have you been, — shall I say so foolish?'

'Yes. Yes. Yes; foolish; — oh yes! But it has been only that. There is nothing, nothing that is not known to all the world. The marvel is that he should not have known it. It was in all the news-papers. But he never thinks of trifles such as that.'

'But why did you keep it from him?'

'Shall I tell you? You know the story of his own engagement.'

'To Miss Tremenhere? Oh yes, I know the story.'

'And how badly she behaved to him, receiving the attention of another man, absolutely while she was engaged to him.'

'She was very pretty; — but a flighty incon-stant little girl. I felt that George had had a great escape.'

'But such was the story. Well; — he told it me.

He told it before he had thought of me. We were together and had become intimate; and out of the full heart the mouth speaks.'

'I can understand that he should have told it you.'

'He did not think of loving me then. Well; — he told me his story, but I kept mine to myself.'

'That was natural, — then.'

'But, when he came to me with the other story and asked me to love him, was I to give him back his own tale and tell him the same thing of myself? I too have had a lover, and I have — jilted him, if you please to call it so. Was I to tell him that?'

'It would hardly have been true, I think.'

'It would have been true, — true to the letter,' said Cecilia, determined that Sir Francis Geraldine's lie should not prevail at this moment. 'I had done to Sir Francis just what the girl had done to your brother. I was guided by other motives and had I think behaved properly. Was I to tell it to him then?'

'Why not?'

'His own story, back again? I could not do it, and then, after that, from time to time the occasions have gone by. Words have been said by him which have made it impossible. Twenty times I have determined to do it, and twenty times the opportunity has been lost. I was obliged to tell this woman not to mention it in his presence.'

'He must know it.'

'I wish he did.'

'He is a man who will not bear to be kept in the dark on such a question.'

'I know it. I have read his character and I know it.'

'You cannot know him as I do,' said Lady Grant. 'Though you are his wife you have not been so long enough to know him; how true he is, how affectionate, how honest; — but yet how jealous. Were I to say that he is unforgiving I should belie him. Without many thoughts he could forgive the man who had robbed him of his fortune, or his health. But it is hard for him to forgive that which he considers to be an offence against his self-love.'

'I know it all.'

'The longer he is kept in the dark the deeper will be the wound. Of such a man it is impossible to say what he suspects. He will not think that you have loved him the less, or that you are less true to him; but there will be something that will rankle, and which he will not endeavour to define. He is the noblest man on earth, and the most generous — till he be offended. But then he is the most bitter.'

'You describe his character just as I have read it.'

'If it be so you must be careful that he learn this from yourself, and not from others. If it come from you he will be angry, that it has come so late. But his anger will pass by and he will forgive you. But if he hears it from the world at large, if it be told of you, and not by you, then I can understand, that his wrath should be very great.'

'Why has he not heard it already?' asked Mrs Western after a pause. 'Why has he not been like all the world who have read it in the newspapers? It was talked of so much, that it was hardly necessary that I should tell it myself.'

'You yourself have said that he does not think of trifles. Paragraphs about the loves and marriages of other people he would never read. You may be sure at any rate of this, — that your engagement with Sir Francis Geraldine he has never read.'

'I have sometimes hoped,' said Mrs Western, 'that he knew it all.' Lady Grant shook her head. 'I have sometimes thought that he knew it all, and regarded it as a matter on which nothing need be said between us. Should I have been angry with him had he not told me of Miss Tremenhere?'

'Do you measure the one thing by the other,' said Lady Grant; 'a man's desires by a woman's, a man's sense of honour by what a woman is supposed to feel? Though a man keep such secrets deep in his bosom through long years of married life, the woman is not supposed to be injured. She may know, or may not know, and may hear the tale at any period of her married life, and no harm will follow. But a man expects to see every thought in the breast of the woman to whose love he trusts, as though it were all written there for him in the clear light, but written in letters which no one else shall read.'

'I have nothing that he may not read,' said Mrs Western.

'But there is something that he has not read, something that he has not been invited to read. Let it not remain so. Tell it to him all even though you may have to support his anger, and for a time to pine in the shadow of his displeasure.'

Mrs Western as she went away to her own room felt some relief at any rate in the conviction that with Lady Grant her secret would be safe. Strong as was the bond which bound her to her brother there would be on her tongue no itching desire to tell the secret simply because it was there to be told. She had not threatened, or spoken of her duty, or boasted of her friendship, but had simply given her advice in the strongest language which it was within her power to use. On the next morning she took her leave, and started on her journey without showing even by a glance that she was possessed of any secret.

'Does she know?' asked Miss Altifiorla as soon as the two were in the drawing-room together, using a kind of whisper which had now become habitual to her.

It may almost be said that Mrs Western had come to hate her friend. She looked forward to the time of her going as a liberation from misery. Miss Altifiorla's intrusion at Durton Lodge was altogether unpalatable to her. She certainly no longer loved her friend, and knew well that her friend knew that it was so. But still she could not risk the open enmity of one who knew her secret. And she was bound to answer the question that was asked her. 'Yes, she does know it.'

'And what does she say?'

'It matters not what she says. My request to you is that you should not speak of it.'

'But to yourself!'

'No, not to myself or to any other person here.' Then she was silent and Miss Altifiorla, pursing up her lips, bethought herself whether the demands made upon her friendship were not too heavy. But there still remained five days of the visit.

Chapter IX

MISS ALTIFIORLA'S DEPARTURE

The fortnight was nearly gone and Miss Altifiorla was to start early on the following morning. Cecilia had resolved that she would tell her story to her husband as soon as they were alone together, and make a clean breast. She would tell him everything down, as far as she could, to the little feelings which had prevented her from speaking before, to Miss Altifiorla's abominable interference, and to Lady Grant's kind advice. She would do this as soon as Miss Altifiorla was out of the house. But she could not quite bring herself to determine on the words she would use. She was resolved, however, that in owning her fault she would endeavour to disarm his wrath by special tenderness. If he were tender; — oh, yes, then she would be tender in return. If he took it kindly then she would worship him. All the agony she endured should be explained to him. Of her own folly she would speak very severely — if he treated it lightly. But she would do nothing to seem to deprecate his wrath. As to all this she was resolved. But she had not yet settled on the words with which she would commence her narrative.

The last day wore itself away very tediously. Miss Altifiorla was in her manner more objectionable than ever. Mr Western had evidently disliked her though he had hardly said so. During the days he had left the two women much together, and had remained in his study or had wandered forth alone. In this way he had increased his wife's feeling of anger against her visitor, and had made her look forward to her departure with increasing impatience. But an event happened which had at once disturbed all her plans. She was sitting in the drawing-room with Miss Altifiorla at about five in the evening, discussing in a most disagreeable manner the secrecy attending her first engagement. That is to say Miss Altifiorla was persisting in the discussion, whereas Mrs Western was positively refusing to make it a subject of conversation. 'I think you are demanding too much from me,' said Miss Altifiorla. 'I have given way, I am afraid wrongly, as to your husband. But I should not do my duty by you were I not to insist on giving you my advice with my last breath. Let me tell it. I shall know how to break the subject to him in a becoming manner.' At this moment the door was opened, and the servant announced Sir Francis Geraldine.

The disturbance of the two women was complete. Had the dead ancestor of either of them been ushered in, they could not have received him with more trepidation. Miss Altifiorla rose with a look of awe, Mrs Western with a feeling of anger that was almost dominated by fear. But neither of them for a moment spoke a word, nor gave any sign of making welcome the new guest.

108

'As I am living so close to you,' said the Baronet, putting on that smile which Mrs Western remembered so well, 'I thought that I was in honour bound to come and renew our acquaintance.'

Mrs Western was utterly unable to speak. 'I don't think that we knew that you were living in the neighbourhood,' said Miss Altifiorla.

'Oh, yes; I have the prettiest, funniest, smallest little cottage in the world just about two miles off. The Criterion it is called.'

'What a very odd name,' said Miss Altifiorla.

'Yes, it is rather odd. I won the race once and bought the place with the money. The horse was called Scratch'em, and I couldn't call my house Scratch'em. I have built a second cottage, so that it is not so very small, and as it is only two miles off I hope that you and Mr Western will come and see it.'

This was addressed exclusively to Cecilia, and made an answer of some kind absolutely necessary. 'I fear that we are going to Scotland very shortly,' she said; 'and my husband is not much in the habit of visiting.'

This was uncivil enough, but Sir Francis did not take it amiss. He sat there for twenty minutes and even made allusion to their former intimacy in Exeter.

'I am quite well aware how happily all that has ended,' he said; — 'at any rate on your side of the question. You have done very well and very wisely. And I,' — he laughed as he said this, —

'have succeeded in getting over it better than might have been expected. At any rate I hope that there will be no ill-will. I shall do myself the honour of asking you and Mr Western to come and dine with me at the Criterion. It is the little place that Lord Tomahawk had last year.' Then he departed without another word from Cecilia Western.

'Now he must be told,' whispered Miss Altifiorla the moment the door was closed. 'My dear, if you will think of it all round you will perceive that this can be done by no one so well as by myself. I will go to Mr Western the moment he comes in, and get through it all in half an hour.'

'You will do nothing of the kind,' said Mrs. Western.

'Let me pray you. Let me implore you. Let me beseech you.'

'You will do nothing of the kind. I will admit of no interference in the matter.'

'Interference! You cannot call it interference.'

'I will not have you speak to my husband on the subject.'

'But what will you do?'

'Whatever I do shall be done by myself alone.'

'But you must tell him instantly. You cannot allow this man to come and call and yet say nothing about it. And he would not have called without some previous acquaintance. This you will have to describe, and if you say that you merely knew him at Exeter, there will be in that case an additional fib.' The use of such words applied to herself by this woman was intolerable. But she could only answer them by an involuntary frown upon her brow. 'And then,' continued Miss Altifiorla, 'of course he will refer to me. He will conclude that as you knew Sir Francis at Exeter I must have known him. I cannot tell a fib.'

She could not tell a fib! And that was uttered in such a way as to declare that Mrs Western had been fibbing. I cannot tell a fib! 'You will leave me at any rate to mind my own business,' said Cecilia in an indignant tone as she left the room.

But Mr Western was at the hall door, and the coming of Sir Francis had to be explained at once. That could not be left to be told when Miss Altifiorla should have gone, — not even though she were going to-morrow. 'Sir Francis Geraldine has been here,' she said almost before he had entered the room. She was immediately aware that she had been too sudden, and had given by her voice too great an importance to her idea of the visit.

But he was not surprised at that and did not notice it. 'Sir Francis Geraldine! A man whom I particularly do not wish to know! And what has brought him here?'

'He came to call. He is a Devonshire man, and he knew us at Exeter.'

'He is the Dean's brother-in-law. I remember. And when he came what did he say? Unless you and he were very intimate I think he might as well have remained away. There are some stories here not altogether to his credit. I do not know much about his business, but he is not a delectable acquaintance.'

'We were intimate,' said Cecilia. 'Maude Hippesley, his niece, was my dearest friend.' The words were no sooner out of her mouth than she was aware that she had fibbed. Miss Altifiorla was justified. Why had she not stopped at the assurance of her intimacy with Sir Francis, and have left unexplained the nature of it? Every step which she took made further steps terribly difficult!

After dinner, Mr Western, as a matter of course, brought up the subject of Sir Francis Geraldine. 'Did you know him, Miss Altifiorla?'

'Oh yes!' said that lady, looking at Cecilia with peculiar eyes. Only that Mr Western was a man and not a woman, and among men the least suspicious till his suspicion were aroused, he would have discovered at once from Miss Altifiorla's manner that there was a secret.

'He seems to have lived in very good clerical society down in Exeter, — a very different class from those with whom he has been intimate here.'

'Of course he was staying at the Deanery,' said Cecilia.

'And he, I know, is a very pearl of Church propriety. It is odd what different colours men show at different places. Down here, where he is well known, a great many even of the racing men fight shy of him. But I beg your pardon if he be a particular friend of yours, Miss Altifiorla.'

'Oh dear no, not of mine at all. I should never have known him to speak to but for Cecilia.' Her words no doubt were true; but again she looked as though endeavouring to tell all she could without breaking her promise.

'He is one of our Devonshire baronets,' said Cecilia, 'and of course we like to stand by our own. At any rate he is going to ask us to dinner.'

'We cannot dine with him.'

'That's as you please. I don't want to dine with him.'

'I look upon it as very impertinent. He knows that I should not dine with him. There has never been any actual quarrel, but there has been no acquaintance.'

'The acquaintance has been on my part,' said Cecilia, who felt that at every word she uttered she made the case worse for herself hereafter.

'When a woman marries, she has to put up with her husband's friends,' said Mr Western gravely.

'He is nothing on earth to me. I never wish to see him again as long as I live.'

'It is unfortunate that he should have turned out to be so near a neighbour,' said Miss Altifiorla. Then for the moment Sir Francis Geraldine was allowed to be forgotten.

'I did not like to say it before her,' he said afterwards in their own room; — and now Cecilia was able to observe that his manner was altogether altered, — 'but to tell the truth that man behaved very badly to me myself. I know nothing about racing, but my cousin, poor Jack Western, did. When he died, there was some money due to him by Sir Francis, and I, as his executor, applied for it. Sir Francis answered that debts won by dead men were not payable. But Jack had been alive when he won this, and it should have been paid before. I know nothing about debts of honour as they are called, but I found out that the money should have been paid.'

'What was the end of it?' asked Cecilia.

'I said no more about it. The money would have come into my pocket and I could afford to lose it. But Sir Francis must know what I think of the transaction, and knowing it ought not to talk of asking me to dinner.'

'But that was swindling.'

'For the matter of that it's all swindling as far as I can see. One strives to get the money out of another man's pocket by some juggling arrangement. For myself I cannot understand how a gentleman can condescend to wish to gain another man's money. But I leave that all alone. It is so; and when I meet a man who is on the turf as they call it, I keep my own feelings to myself. He has his own laws of conduct and I have mine. But here is a man who does not obey his own laws; and puts money in his pocket by breaking them. He can do as he pleases. It is nothing to me. But he ought not to come and call upon my wife.' In this way he talked himself into a passion; but the passion was now against Sir Francis Geraldine and not against his wife.

On the next morning Miss Altifiorla was dispatched by an early train so that she might be able to get down to Exeter, via London, early in the day. It behoved her to go to London on the route. She had things to buy and people to see, and to London she went. 'Good-bye, my dear,' she said, seeming to include the husband as well as the wife in the address. 'I have spent a most pleasant fortnight, and have been most delighted to become acquainted with your husband. You are Cecilia Holt no longer. But it would have been sad indeed not to know him who has made you Cecilia Western.' Then she put out her hand, and getting hold of that of the gentleman squeezed it with the warmest affection. But her farewell address made to Mrs Western in her own room was quite different in its tone. 'Now I am going, Cecilia,' she said, 'and am leaving you in the midst of terrible danger.'

'I hope not,' said Cecilia.

'But I am. It would have been over now and passed if you would have allowed me to obey my reason, and to tell him the whole story of your former love.'

'Why you?'

'Because I am your most intimate friend. And I think I should have told it in such a manner as to disarm his wrath.'

'It is out of the question. I will tell him.'

'Do so. Do so. But I doubt your courage. Do

so this very morning. And remember that at any rate Francesca Altifiorla has been true to her promise.'

That such a promise should have been needed and should have been boasted of with such violent vulgarity was almost more than Mrs Western could stand. She came down-stairs and then underwent the additional purgatory of listening to the silver-tongued farewell. That she, she with her high ideas of a woman's duty and a woman's dignity, should have put herself into such a condition was a marvel to herself. Had some one a year since told her that she should become thus afraid of a fellow-creature and of one that she loved best in all the world she would have repelled him who had told her with disdain. But so it was. How was she to tell her husband that she had been engaged to one whom he had described to her as a gambler and a swindler?

Chapter X

SIR FRANCIS TRAVELS WITH MISS ALTIFIORLA

Miss Altifiorla was at the station of course before her time. It is the privilege of unmarried ladies when they travel alone to spend a good deal of time at stations. But as she walked up and down the platform she had an opportunity for settling her thoughts. She was angry with three persons, with Mrs Western, Mr Western, and with herself. She was very angry with Cecilia. Had Cecilia trusted to her properly she could have sympathised with her thoroughly in all her troubles. She was not angry with her friend in that her friend was afraid of her husband. Would she have reposed herself and her fears on her friend's bosom it might have been very well. But it was because her friend had not been afraid of her that she was wroth. Mrs Western had misbehaved egregiously and had come to her in her trouble solely because it was necessary. So far she had done naturally. But though she had come, she had not come in any of the spirit of humility. She had been bold as brass to her in the midst of her cowardice towards her husband, — imperious to herself and unbending. She had declined her advice with scorn. And yet one word spoken by herself would have been destructive. Seeing that she had been so treated had she not been wrong to abstain from the word?

Her anger against Mr Western was less hot in its nature but was still constant. He had not liked her, and though he had been formally civil his dislike had been apparent. He was a man proud of himself, who ought to be punished for his pride. It was quite proper that he should learn that his wife had been engaged to the man whom he had so violently despised. It would be no more than a fitting reverse of fortune. Mr Western was she thought no better than other men and ought to be made so to understand. She had not quite arranged in her mind what she could now do in the matter, but for 'dear Cecilia's' sake she was sure that something must be done.

And she was angry with herself at allowing herself to be turned out of the house before the crisis had come. She felt that she ought to have been present at the crisis and that by the exercise of her own powers she might have hurried on the crisis. In this respect she was by no means satisfied with herself.

She was walking up and down the platform of the little country station thinking of all this when on a sudden she saw Sir Francis Geraldine get out of a brougham. It cannot be explained why her heart throbbed when she saw Sir Francis get out of his brougham. It was not that she thought that she could ask his advice on the matters which filled her mind, but there probably did come to her vague ideas of the possibility of some joint action. At any rate she received him when he came upon the platform with her blandest smile, and immediately entered into conversation with him respecting the household of the Westerns. What a stiff man he was, so learned, so proper, and so distant! It was impossible to get on with him. No doubt he was very good and all that. But what was their poor dear Cecilia to do with a man so silent, and one who hated all amusements? Before the train came up she and Sir Francis were quite on good terms together; and as they were both going to London they got into the same carriage.

'Of course he's a prig,' said Sir Francis, as they seated themselves opposite to one another. 'But then his wife is a prig too, and I do not see why they should not suit each other.'

'You did not use to think her a prig, Sir Francis.'

'No; like other men I made a mistake and was nearly having to pay for it. But I discovered in time, — luckily for both of us.'

'You know,' said Miss Altifiorla, 'that Cecilia Holt was my dearest friend, and I cannot endure to hear her abused.'

'Abused! You do not think I wish to abuse her. I am awfully fond of her still. But I do not see why she and Western should not get on very well together. I suppose they've no secrets from each other,' he added after a pause. Upon this Miss Altifiorla remained silent. 'They tell each other everything I should think.' Still Miss Altifiorla said nothing. 'I should imagine that she would tell him everything.'

'Upon my word I can't say.'

'I suppose she does. About her former engagement for instance. He knows the whole story,
eh?'

'I declare you put it to me in such a way that
one doesn't know how to answer you.'

'Different people have such different opinions
about these kind of things. Some people think
that because a girl has been engaged to a man
she never ought to speak to him again when the
engagement is broken. For my part I do not see
why they should not be as intimate as any other
people. She looked at me the other day as though
she thought that I ought not to put myself into
the same room with her again. I suppose she did
it in obedience to him.'

What was Miss Altifiorla to say in answer to
such a question? She did remember her promise,
and her promise was in a way binding upon her.
She wished so to keep it as to be able to boast
that she had kept it. But still she was most anxious to break it in the spirit. She did understand
that she had bound herself not to divulge aught
about Mrs Western's secret, and that were she to
do so now to Sir Francis she would be untrue to
her friend. But the provocation was strong; and
she felt that Sir Francis was a man with whom it
would be pleasant to form an alliance.

'You must know,' said Sir Francis.

'I don't see that I need know at all. Of course
Cecilia does tell me everything; but I do not see

that for that reason I am bound to tell any one else.'

'Then you do know.'

'Know what?'

'Has she told him that she was engaged to me? Or does he not know it without her telling him?' By this time they had become very intimate and were whispering backwards and forwards with each other at their end of the carriage. All this was very pleasant to Miss Altifiorla. She felt that she was becoming the recipient of an amount of confidential friendship which had altogether been refused to her during the last two weeks. Sir Francis was a baronet, and a man of fashion, and a gentleman very well thought of in Devonshire, let Mr Western say what he might about his conduct. Mr Western was evidently a stiff stern man who did not like the amusements of other gentlemen. Miss Altifiorla felt that she liked being the friend of a man of fashion, and she despised Mr Western. She threw herself back on the seat and closed her eyes and laughed. But he pressed her with the same question in another form. 'Does he know that she was engaged to me?'

'If you will ask me, I do not think that he does.'

'You really mean to say that he had never heard of it before his marriage?'

'What am I to do when you press me in this way? Remember that I do not tell you anything of my own knowledge. It is only what I think.'

'You just now said that she told you everything.'

'But perhaps she doesn't know herself.'

'At any rate there is a mystery about it.'

'I think there is, Sir Francis.' After that it was not very long before Miss Altifiorla was induced to talk with great openness of the whole affair, and before they had reached London she had divulged to Sir Francis the fact that Mrs Western had as yet told her husband nothing of her previous engagement, and lived at the present moment in awe at the idea of having to do so. 'I had no conception that Cecilia would have been such a coward,' she said, as Sir Francis was putting her into a cab, 'but such is the sad fact. She has never mentioned your name.'

'And was therefore dreadfully frightened when I called.'

'Oh dreadfully! But I shouldn't wonder if she has told him all about it now.'

'Already, you think.' He was standing at the door of the cab, detaining it, and thereby showing in a very pleasant manner the importance of the interview.

'Well; — I cannot say. Perhaps not yet. She had certainly not made the communication when I left this morning, but was only waiting for my departure to do so. So she said at least. But she is terribly afraid of him and perhaps has not plucked up her courage. But I must be off now.'

'When do you leave town?'

'This afternoon. You are delaying me terribly at this moment. Don't, Sir Francis!' This she said in a whisper because he had got hold of her hand through the window, as though to say good-bye to her, and did not at once let it go.

'When do you go? I'll see you off by the other train. When do you go, and from where?'

'Will you though? That will be very kind. Waterloo; — at 4.30. Remember the 4.30.'

'Sans adieu!' Then she kissed her hand to him and was driven off.

This to her was all very pleasant. It gave an instant rose colour to her life. She had achieved such a character down at Exeter for maidenly reserve, and had lived so sternly, that it was hardly in her memory that a man had squeezed her hand before. She did remember one young clergyman who had sinned in this direction, twelve years since, but he was now a Bishop. When she heard the other day that he had been made a Bishop some misgivings as to her great philosophy touched her mind. Had she done right in repudiating mankind? Would it not have been better now to have been driving about the streets of the episcopal city, or perhaps even those of the metropolis, in an episcopal carriage? But as she had then said she had chosen her line and must now abide by it. But the pressing of her hand by Sir Francis had opened up new ideas to her. And they were the pleasanter because a special arrangement had been made for their meeting once again before they left London. As to one point she was quite determined. Mrs Western and her secret must be altogether discarded. As for her promise she had not really broken it. He had been clever enough to extract from her all that she knew without, as she thought, any positive statement on her own part. At any rate he did know the truth, and no concealment could any longer be of service to Cecilia. It was evident that the way was open to her now and that she could tell all that she knew without any breach of confidence.

Sir Francis, when he left her, was quite determined to carry his project through. Cecilia had thrown him over with most abominable unconcern and self-sufficiency. He had intended to honour her and she had monstrously dishonoured him. He had endeavoured to escape this by taking upon himself falsely the fault of having been the first to break their engagement. But there was a doubt as to this point, and people said that he had been jilted — much to his disgust. He was determined to be revenged, — or as he said to himself, 'he had made up his mind that the broad truth should be known.' It certainly would be the 'broad truth' if he could make Mr Western understand the relations on which he, Sir Francis, had but a few months before stood in regard to his wife. 'Honesty,' he said to himself, 'demanded it.'

Miss Altifiorla, he thought, was by no means an unpleasant young woman with whom to have an intrigue. She had good looks of her own, though they were thin and a little pinched. She was in truth thirty-five years old, but she did not quite look it. She had a certain brightness of eye when she was awakened to enthusiasm, and she knew how to make the best of herself. She could whisper and be — or pretend to be secret. She had about her, at her command to assume, a great air of special friendship. She had not practised it much with men as yet, but there was no reason why she should not do so with advantage. She felt herself already quite on intimate terms with Sir Francis; and of Sir Francis it may be said, that he was sufficiently charmed with Miss Altifiorla to find it expedient to go and see her off from the Waterloo Station.

He found Dick Ross at his club and lunched with him. 'You're just up from the Criterion,' said Dick.

'Yes; I went down for the sake of renewing an old acquaintance, and I renewed it.'

'You've been persecuting that unfortunate young woman.'

'Why a young woman should be thought unfortunate because she marries such a pink of perfection as Mr Western, and avoids such a scapegrace as I am, I cannot conceive.'

'She's unfortunate because you mean to bully her. Why can't you leave her alone? She has had her chance of war, and you have had yours, and he has had his. As far as I can see you have had the best of it. She is married to a stiff prig of a fellow, who no doubt will make her miserable. Surely that ought to be enough for you.'

'Not quite,' said Sir Francis. 'There is nothing

recommends itself to my mind so much as even-handed justice. He played me a trick once, and I'll play him another. She too played me a trick, and now I can play her one. My good fortune consists in this, that I can kill the two birds with one stone.'

'You mean to kill them?'

'Certainly I do. Why on earth should I let them off? He did not let me off. Nor did she. They think because I carry things in an easy manner that I take them easily. I suffer as much as they do. But they shall suffer as well as I.'

'The most pernicious doctrine I ever heard in my life,' said Dick Ross as he filled his mouth with cold chicken pie.

'When you say pernicious, have you any idea what you mean?'

'Well, yes; awfully savage, and all that kind of thing. Just utter cruelty, and a bad spirit.'

'Those are your ideas because you don't take the trouble to return evil for evil. But then you never take the trouble to return good for good. In fact, you have no idea of duty, only you don't like to burden your conscience with doing what seems to be ill-natured. Now, if a man does me good, I return it, — which I deem to be a great duty, and if he does me evil, I generally return that sooner or later. There is some idea of justice in my conduct, but there is none in yours.'

'Do you mean to punish them both?'

'Well, yes; as far as it is in my power, both.'

'Don't,' said Dick Ross, looking up with

something like real sorrow depicted on his face. But still he called for some greengage pie.

'I like to get the better of my enemies,' said the Baronet. 'You like fruit pie. I doubt if you'd even give up fruit pie to save this woman.'

'I will,' said Dick, pushing the pie away from him.

'The sacrifice would be all in vain. I must write the letter to-day, and as it has to be thought about I must begin it at once. Whatever happens, do not let your good nature quarrel with your appetite.'

'He's a fiend, a perfect fiend,' said Dick Ross, as he sat dawdling over his cheese. 'I wouldn't have his ill-nature for all his money.' But he turned that sentiment over in his mind, endeavouring to ascertain what he would do if the offer of the exchange were made to him. For Dick was very poor, and at this moment was in great want of money. Sir Francis went into the smoking-room, and sitting there alone with a cigar in his mouth, meditated the letter which he would have to write. The letter should be addressed to Mr Western, and was one which could not be written without much forethought. He not only must tell his story, but must give some reason more or less plausible for the telling of it. He did not think that he could at once make his idea of justice plain to Mr Western. He could not put forth his case so clearly as to make the husband understand that all was done in fair honour and honesty. But as he thought of it, he came to the conclusion that he did not much care what impression he might leave on the mind of Mr Western; — and still less what impression he might leave on hers. He might probably succeed in creating a quarrel, and he was of opinion that Mr Western was a man who would not quarrel lightly, but, when he did, would quarrel very earnestly. Having thought it all over with great deliberation, he went up-stairs, and in twenty minutes had his letter written. At a quarter past four he was at the Waterloo Station to see the departure of Miss Altifiorla. Even he could perceive that she was somewhat brighter in her attire than when he had met her early in the morning. He could not say what had been done, but something had been added to please his eyes. The gloves were not the same, nor the ribbons; and he thought that he perceived that even the bonnet had been altered. Her manner too was changed. There was a careless ease and freedom about her which he rather liked; and he took it in good part that Miss Altifiorla had prepared herself for the interview, though he were to be with her but for a few minutes, and that she should be different from the Miss Altifiorla, as she had come away from the Western breakfast table. 'Now there is one thing I want you to promise me,' she said as she gave him her hand.

'Anything on earth.'

'Don't let Mr Western or Cecilia know what you know about that.' He laughed and merely shook his head. 'Pray don't. What's the good?

You'll only create a disturbance and misery. Poor dear Cecilia has been uncommonly silly. But I don't think that she deserves to be punished quite so severely.'

'I'm afraid I must differ from you there,' he said, shaking his head.

'Is it absolutely necessary?'

'Absolutely.'

'Poor Cecilia! How can she have been so foolish! He is of such a singular temperament that I do not know what the effect may be. I wish you would think better of it, Sir Francis.'

'And leave myself to stand in my present very uncomfortable position! And that after such treatment as hers. I have thought it all over, and have found myself bound in honour to inform him. And it is for the sake of letting you know that I have come here. Perhaps you may be called upon to say or do something in the matter.'

'I suppose it cannot be helped,' said Miss Altifiorla with a sigh.

'It cannot,' he replied.

'Poor dear Cecilia. She has brought it on her own head. I must get into my train now, as we are just off. I am so much obliged to you for coming to see me start.'

'We shall meet each other before long,' he said, as she again kissed her hand and took her departure. Miss Altifiorla could not but think what a happy chance it was that prevented his marriage with Cecilia Holt.

Chapter XI

MR WESTERN
HEARS THE STORY

It was the custom for Mr Western to come down into the library before breakfast, and there to receive his letters. On the morning after Miss Altifiorla's departure he got one by which it may be said that he was indeed astonished. It can seldom be the case that a man shall receive a letter by which he is so absolutely lifted out of his own world of ordinary contentment into another absolutely different. And the world into which he was lifted was one black with unintelligible storms and clouds. It was as though everything were suddenly changed for him. The change was of a nature which altogether unmanned him. Had he been ruined that would have been as nothing in comparison. The death of no friend, — so he told himself in the first moment of his misery, — could have so afflicted him. He read the letter through twice and thrice, and then sat silent with it in his hand thinking of it. There could be but one relief, but that relief must surely be forthcoming. The letter could not be true. How to account for its falsehood, how to explain to himself that such a letter should have been written to him without any foundation for it, without any basis on which such a story could be constructed, he could not imagine to himself. But he resolved not to believe it. He saw that were he to believe it, and to have believed it wrongly, the offence given would be ineffable. He should never dare to look his wife in the face again. It was at any rate infinitely safer for him to disbelieve it. He sat there mute, immovable, without a change of countenance, without even a frown on his brow, for a quarter of an hour: and at the end of that time he got up and shook himself. It was not true. Whatever might be the explanation, it could not be true. There was some foul plot against his happiness; but whatever the nature of the plot might be, he was sure that the story as told to him in that letter was not true. And yet it was with a very heavy heart that he rose and walked off to his wife's room.

The letter ran as follows: —

'MY DEAR MR WESTERN, — I think it is necessary that I should allude to a former little incident in my past life, — one that took place in the course of the last year only, — to account for the visit which I made to your house the other day, and which was not, I think, very well taken. I have no reason to doubt but that you are acquainted with all the circumstances. Indeed I look upon it as impossible that you should not be so. But, taking that for granted, I have to explain my own conduct.

'It seems but the other day that Cecilia Holt and I were engaged to be married.' Mr Western, when he came to this passage, felt for a moment as though he had received a bullet in his heart. 'All Exeter knew of the engagement, and all Exeter seemed to be well pleased. I was staying with my brother-in-law, the Dean, and had found Miss Holt very intimate at the Deanery. It is not for me now to explain the way in which our engagement was broken through, but your wife, I do not doubt, in telling you of the affair, will have stated that she did not consider herself to have been ill-used. I am quite certain that she can never have said so even to herself. I do not wish to go into the matter in all its details, but I am confident that she cannot have complained of me.

'Under these circumstances, when I found myself living close to you, and to her also, I thought it better to call and to offer such courtesies as are generally held to be pleasant in a neighbourhood. It would, I thought, be much pleasanter to meet in that frank way than to go on cutting each other, especially as there was no ground for a quarrel on either side. I have, however, learned since that something has been taken amiss. What is it? If it be that I was before you, that is too late to be mended. You, at any rate, have won the prize, and ought to be contented. You also were engaged about the same time, and my cousin has got your young lady. It is I that was left out in the cold, and I really do not see that you have any reason to be angry. I have no wish to force myself upon you, and if you do not wish to be gracious down at Ascot, then let there be an end of it.

'Yours truly,
'FRANCIS GERALDINE.'

He arose and went slowly up-stairs to his wife's bedroom. It was just the time when she would come down to breakfast and as his hand was on the lock of the door she opened it to come out. The moment she saw him she knew that her secret had been divulged. She knew that he knew it, and yet he had endeavoured to eradicate all show of anger from his face, as all reality of it from his heart. He was sure, — was sure, — that the story was an infamous falsehood! His wife, his chosen one, his Cecilia to have been engaged, a year ago, to such a one as Sir Francis Geraldine, — to so base, so mean a creature, — and then to have married him without telling a word of it all! To have kept him wilfully, carefully, in the dark, with studied premeditation so as to be sure of effecting her own marriage before he should learn it, and that too when he had told her everything as to himself! It certainly could not be, and was not true!

She stood still holding the door open when she saw him there with the letter in his hand. There was an instant certainty that the blow had come and must be borne even should it kill her. It was as though she were already crushed by the weight of it. Her own conduct appeared to her black with all its enormity. Though there had been so little done by her which was really amiss, yet she felt that she had been guilty beyond the reach of pardon. Twelve months since she could have declared that she knew herself so well as to be sure that she could never tremble before any one. But all that was changed with her. Her very nature was changed. She felt as though she were a guilty, discovered, and disgraced criminal. She stood perfectly still, looking him in the face, but without a word.

And he! His perceptions were not quick as hers, and he still was determined to disbelieve. 'Cecilia!' he said, 'I have got a letter.' And he passed on into the room. She followed him and stood with her hand resting on the shoulder of the sofa. 'I have got a letter from Sir Francis Geraldine.'

'What does Sir Francis Geraldine say of me?' she replied.

Had he been a man possessed of quick wit, he would have perceived now that the letter was true. There was confession in the very tone of her voice. But he had come there determined that it was not true, determined at any rate to act as though it were not true; and it was necessary that he should go through the game as he had arranged to play it. 'It is a base letter,' he said. 'A foul lying letter. But there is some plot in it of which I know nothing. You can perhaps explain the plot.'

'Maybe the letter is true,' she said standing

there, not submissive before him, but still utterly miserable in her guilt.

'It is untrue. It cannot possibly be true. It contains a wicked lie. He says that twelve months since you were engaged to him as his wife. Why does he lie like that?' She stood before him quite quiet without the change of a muscle of her face. 'Do you understand the meaning of it all?'

'Oh, yes.'

'What is the meaning? Speak to me and explain it.'

'I was engaged to marry Sir Francis Geraldine just before I knew you. It was broken off and then we went upon the Continent. There I met you. Oh, George, I have loved you so well. I do love you so truly.' As she spoke she endeavoured to take his hand in hers. She made that one effort to be tender in obedience to her conscience, but as she made it she knew that it would be in vain.

He rejected her hand, without violence indeed but still with an assured purpose, and walked away from her to the further side of the chamber. 'It is true then?'

'Yes; it is true. Why should it not be true?'

'Heaven help us! And I to hear about it for the first time in such a fashion as this! He comes to see you, and because something does not go as he would have it, he turns round and tells me his story. But that he has quarrelled with you now, I should never have heard a syllable.' He had come up to her room determined not to believe a word of it. And now, suddenly, there was no fault of which in his mind he was not ready to accuse her. He had been deceived, and she was to him a thing altogether different from that which he had believed her.

But she, too, was stung to wrath by the insinuation which his words contained. She knew herself to be absolutely innocent in every respect, except that of reticence to her husband. Though she was prepared to bear the weight of the punishment to which her silence had condemned her, yet she was sure of the purity of her own conduct. Knowing his disposition, she did not care to make light of her great fault, but now something was added, she hardly knew what, of which she knew herself to be innocent. Something was hinted as to the friendship remaining between her and this man, of which her husband, in his pride, should not have accused her. What! Did he think that she had willingly received her late lover as her friend in his house and without his knowledge? If he thought that, then, indeed, must all be over between them. 'I do not know what it is that you suspect. You had better say it out at once.'

'Is this letter true?' and he held the letter up in his hand.

'I suppose it to be true. I do not know what it contains, but I presume it to be true.'

'You can read it,' and he threw the letter on the table before her.

She took it up and slowly passed her eyes over the words, endeavouring, as she did, to come to some determination as to what her conduct should be. The purport of the words she did not fully comprehend, so fully was her mind occupied with thinking of the condition of her husband's mind; but they left upon her an impression that in the main Sir Francis Geraldine had told his story truly. 'Yes;' she said, 'it is true. Before I had met you I was engaged to marry this other man. Our engagement was broken off, and then mamma and I travelled abroad together. We there met you and then you know the rest.'

'And you thought it proper that I should be kept in the dark!' She remained silent. She could not apologise to him after hearing the accusation which rankled in his bosom. She could not go on to explain that the moment fittest for an explanation had never come. She could not endeavour even to make him understand that because her story was so like his own, hers had not been told. She knew the comparative insignificance of her own fault, and yet circumstances had brought it about that she must stand oppressed with this weight of guilt in her eyes. As he should be just or unjust, or rather merciful or unmerciful, so must she endure or be unable to endure her doom. 'I do not understand it,' he said, with affected calm. 'It is the case, then, that you have brought me into this position with premeditated falsehood, and have wilfully deceived me as to your previous engagement?'

'No!'

'How then?'

'There has been no wilful deceit, — no cause for deceit whatsoever. You were engaged to marry the lady who is now Mrs Geraldine. I was engaged to marry Sir Francis.'

'But I told you all.'

'You did.'

'It would have been impossible that I should have asked you to be mine without telling you the whole story.' She could not answer him. She knew it to be true, — that he had told her and must have told her. But for herself it had been so improbable that he had not known of her engagement! And then there had been no opportunity, — no fitting opportunity. She knew that she had been wrong, foolish, ill-judging; but there had been nothing of that premeditated secrecy, — that secrecy with a cause, of which he had hinted that she was guilty. 'I suppose that I may take it as proved that I have been altogether mistaken?' This he said in the severest tone which he knew how to assume.

'How mistaken?'

'I have believed you to be sweet, and pure, and innocent, and true; — one in whom my spirit might refresh itself as a man bathes his heated limbs in the cool water. You were to have been to me the joy of my life, — my great treasure kept at home, open to no eyes but my own; a thing perfect in beauty, to think of when absent and to be conscious of when present, without even the need of expression. "Let the wind come and the storm," I said to myself, "I cannot be unhappy, because my wife is my own." There is an external grace about you which was to my thinking only the culture of the woman within.'

'Well; — well.'

'It was a dream. I had better have married that little girl. She was silly, and soon loved some one better. But she did not deceive me.'

'And I, — have I deceived you?'

He paused before he answered her, and then spoke as though with much thought, 'Yes,' he said; 'yes.'

'Where? How?'

'I do not know. I cannot pretend even to guess. I shall probably never know. I shall not strive to know. But I do know that you have deceived me. There has been, nay, there is, a secret between you and one whom I regard as among the basest of men, of which I have been kept purposely in ignorance.'

'There is no such secret.'

'You were engaged to be his wife. That at any rate has been kept from me. He has been here as your friend, and when he came, — into my house, — the purport of his visit was kept from me. He asked for something, which was refused, and consequently he has written to me. For what did he ask?'

'Ask! For nothing! What was there for him to ask?'

'I do not know. I cannot even pretend to guess. As I read his letter there must have been something. But it does not matter. While you have seemed to me to be one thing, you have been another. You have been acting a part from the first moment in which we met, and kept it up all through with admirable consistency. You are not that sweetly innocent creature which I have believed you to be.'

She knew that she was all that he had fancied her, but she could not say so. She had understood him thoroughly when he had told her that she had been to him the cool water in which the heated man had bathed his limbs; that she was the treasure to be kept at home. Even in her misery something of delight had come to her senses as she heard him say that. The position described to her had been exactly that which it had been her ambition to fill. She knew that in spite of all that had come and gone she was still fit to fill it. There had been nothing, — not a thought to mar her innocence, her purity, her woman's tenderness. She was all his, and he was certain to know every thought of her mind and every throb of her heart. She did believe that if he could read them all, he would be perfectly satisfied. But she could not tell him that it was so. Words so spoken will be the sweetest that can fall into a man's ear, — if they be believed. But let there come but the shadow of a doubt over the man's mind, let him question the sincerity of a tone, and the words will become untrue, mawkish and distasteful. A thing perfect in beauty! How was she to say that she would be that to him? And yet, understanding her error as she had done with a full intelligence, she could have sworn that it should be so. The beauty he had spoken of was not simply the sheen of her loveliness, nor the grace of her form. It was the entirety of her feminine attraction, including the purity of her soul, which was in truth still there in all its perfection. But she could not tell him that he was mistaken in doubting her. Now he had told her that she was not that innocent creature which he had believed her to be. What was she to do? How was she to restore herself to his favour? But through it all there was present to her an idea that she would not humble herself too far. To the extent of the sin which she had committed she would humble herself if she knew how to do that without going beyond it. But further than that in justice both to him and to herself she would not go. 'If you have condemned me,' she said, 'there must be an end of it, — for the present.'

'Condemned you! Do you not condemn yourself? Have you attempted any word of excuse? Have you given any reason why I should have been kept in the dark? Your friend Miss Altifiorla knew it all I presume?'

'Yes, she knew it all.'

'And you would not have had her here if you could have avoided it lest she should tell me?'

'That is true. I wished to be the first to tell you myself.'

'And yet you had never whispered a word of it. Miss Altifiorla and Sir Francis it seems are friends.' Cecilia only shook her head. 'I heard yesterday at the station that they had gone to London together. I presume they are friends.'

Quickly the idea passed through Mrs Western's mind that Miss Altifiorla had been untrue to her. She had kept her word to the letter in not having told the secret to her husband but she had discussed the whole matter with Sir Francis, and the letter which Sir Francis had written was the result. 'I do not know,' she said. 'If they be more to each other than chance acquaintance I do not know it. From week to week and from day to day before our marriage the thing went on and the opportunity never came. Something would always fall from you which made me afraid to speak at that moment. Then we were married, and I found how wrong I had been. I still re-solved to tell you, but put it off like a coward from day to day. Your sister had heard of my first engagement.'

'Did Bertha know it?'

'Yes; and like myself she was surprised that you should be so ignorant.'

'She might well be surprised.'

'Then I resolved to tell you. I would not do it till that other woman had left the house. I would not have her by to see your anger.'

'And now this is the way in which the history of your former life has reached my ears!' As he said this he held out in his hand the fatal letter. 'This is the manner in which you have left me to be informed of a subject so interesting! I first hear from Sir Francis Geraldine that he and you a twelvemonth since were engaged together as man and wife.' Here she stood quite silent. She did not care to tell him that it was more than twelve months since. 'That you think to be becoming.'

'I do not think so.'

'That you feel to be compatible with my happiness!' Here, again, there was a pause, during which she looked fully into his face. 'Such is not my idea. My happiness is wrecked. It is gone.' Here he made a motion with his hand, as though to show that all his bliss had flown away from him.

'Oh George, if you love me, do not speak like that.'

'Love you! Yes, I love you. I do not suppose that love can be made to go at once, as I find that esteem may do, and respect, and veneration.'

'Oh, George, those are hard words.'

'Is it not so? This morning you were to me of all God's creatures the brightest and the best. When I entered your room just now it was so that I regarded you. Can you now be the brightest and the best? Has not all that romance been changed at a moment's notice? But alas! love does not go after the same fashion.' Then he turned shortly round and left the room.

She remained confounded and awe-stricken. There had been that about him which seemed to declare a settled purpose — as though he had intended to leave her for ever. She sat perfectly still thinking of it, thinking of the injustice of the sentence that had been pronounced upon her. Though she had deserved much she had not deserved this. Though she had expected punishment she had not expected punishment so severe. In about twenty minutes her maid came up to her, and with a grave face asked whether she would wish that breakfast should be sent to her in her own room. Mr Western had sent to ask the question. 'Yes,' said she, — 'if he pleases.' There could be no good in attempting to conceal from the servants a misery so deep and so lasting as this.

Chapter XII

MR WESTERN'S DECISION

What should she do with herself? Her breakfast was brought to her. At noon she was told that Mr Western had gone out for the day and would not return till the evening. She was asked whether she would have her pony carriage, and on refusing it, was persuaded by her maid to walk in the grounds. 'I think I will go out,' she said, and went and walked for an hour. Her maid had been peculiarly her own and had come to her from Exeter; but she would not talk to her maid about her quarrel with her husband, though she was sure that the girl knew of the quarrel. Those messages had certainly come direct from her husband, and could not, she thought, have been sent without some explanation of the facts. She could see on the faces of all the household that every one knew that there was a quarrel. Twenty times during the day would she have had her husband's name on her tongue had there been no quarrel. It had been with her as though she had had a pride in declaring herself to be his wife. But now she was silent respecting him altogether. She would not bring herself to ask the gardener whether Mr Western wished this thing or the other. The answer had always been that the master wished the paths and the shrubs and the flowers to be just

145

as she wished them. But now not a word was spoken. For an hour she walked among the paths, and then returned to her own room. Would she have her dinner in the dining-room? If so, the master would have his in the library. Then she could restrain herself no longer, but burst into tears. No; she would have no dinner. Let them bring her a cup of tea in her own room.

There she sat thinking of her condition, wondering from hour to hour what was to be the end of it. From hour to hour she sat, and can hardly have been said to think. She lost herself in pondering first over her own folly and then upon his gross injustice. She could not but marvel at her own folly. She had in truth known from the first moment in which she had resolved to accept his offer, that it was her duty to tell him the story of her adventure with Sir Francis Geraldine. It should have been told indeed before she had accepted his offer, and she could not now forgive herself in that she had been silent. 'You must know my story,' she should have said, 'before there can be a word more spoken between us.' And then with a clear brow and without a tremor in her voice she could have told it. But she had allowed herself to be silent, simply because he had told the same story, and then the moment had never come. She could not forgive herself. She could never entirely forgive herself, even though the day should come in which he might pardon her.

But would he ever pardon her? Then her mind

would fly away to the injustice of his condemnation. He had spoken to her darkly, as though he had intended to accuse her of some secret understanding with Sir Francis. He had believed her to be guilty of some underhand plot against his happiness carried on with the man to whom she had been engaged! Of what was it that he had imagined her to be guilty? What was the plot of which in his heart he accused her? Then her imagination looked out and seemed to tell her that there could be but one. Her husband suspected her of having married him while her heart was still the property of that other man! And as she thought of this, indignation for the time almost choked her grief. Could it be possible that he, to whom she had given everything with such utter unreserve, whom she had made the god of her idolatry, to whom she had been exactly that which he had known so well how to describe, — could it be that he should have had every thought concerning her changed in a moment, and that from believing her to be all pure and all innocent, he should have come to regard her as a thing so vile as that? She almost tore her hair in her agony as she said that it must be so. He had told her that his respect, his esteem, and his veneration, had all passed away. She could never consent to live with him trusting solely to his love without esteem.

But as the evening passed away and the night came, and as the duration of the long hours of the day seemed to grow upon her, and as no tidings came to her from her lord, she began to tell herself that it was unbecoming that she should remain without knowing her fate. The whole length of the tedious day had passed since he had left her and had condemned her to breakfast in solitude. Then she accused herself of having been hard with him during that interview, of having failed to submit herself in repentance, and she told herself that if she could see him once more, she might still whisper to him the truth and soften his wrath. But something she must do. She had dismissed her maid for the last time, and sat miserably in her room till midnight. But still she could not go to bed till she had made some effort. She would at any rate write to him one word. She got up therefore and seated herself at the table with pen and ink before her. She would write the whole story, she thought, simply the whole story, and would send it to him, leaving it to him to believe or to disbelieve it as he pleased. But as she bent over the table she felt that she could not write such a letter as that without devoting an entire day to it. Then she rapidly scrawled a few words: —

'DEAREST GEORGE, — Come to me and let me tell you everything. Your own CECILIA.'

Then she addressed it to him and put it under her pillow that she might send it to him as soon as she should wake in the morning. Having done so she got into her bed and wept herself asleep.

When the girl came into her room in the morning she at once asked after her husband. 'Is Mr Western up yet?' The maid informed her with an air of grave distress that Mr Western had risen early and had been driven away from the house to catch a morning train. More than that the girl could not say. But she believed that a letter had been left on the library table. She had heard John say that there was such a letter. But John had gone with his master to the station. Then she sent down for the letter, and within a few minutes held it in her hand.

We will now go back to Mr Western. He, as soon as he had left his wife's room in the morning went downstairs, and began to consider within himself what was the cause of this evil thing which had been done to him. A very evil thing had been done. He did feel that the absolute happiness which had been his for the last few days had perished and gone from him. He was a man undemonstrative, and silent in expressing his own feelings, but one who revelled inwardly in his own feelings of contentment when he was content. His wife had been to him all that he had dreamt that a woman should be. She had filled up his cup with infinite bliss, though he had never told even to her how full his cup had been. But in everything he had striven to gratify her, and had been altogether successful. To go on from day to day with his books, with his garden, with his exercise, and above all with his wife, had been enough to secure absolute happiness. He had suspected no misfortune, and had anticipated no drawback. Then on a sudden there had come this wicked letter, which had made him wretched for the time, even though he were sure that it was not true. But he had known that it was only for the time, for he had been sure that it was untrue. Then the blow had fallen, and all his contentment was banished. There was some terrible mystery, — some mystery of which he could not gauge the depth. Though he was gracious and confiding and honest when left at peace, still he was painfully suspicious when something arose of which the circumstances were kept back from him. There was a secret here, — there was certainly a secret; and it was shared between his wife, whom of all human beings he had loved the best, and the man whom he most thoroughly despised. As long as it was possible that the whole tale might be an invention he would not believe a word against his wife; but, when it appeared that there was certainly some truth in it, then it seemed that there was nothing too monstrous for him to believe.

After his solitary breakfast he walked abroad, and turned it all over in his mind. He had given her the opportunity of telling him everything, and she had told him nothing. So he declared to himself. That one condemning fact was there, — clear as daylight, that she had willingly bestowed herself upon this baronet, this creature who to his thinking was vile as a man could be. As to that there was no doubt. That was declared.

How different must she have been from that creature whom he had fancied that he had loved, when she would have willingly consented to be the wife of such a man? And this had been done within a year, — as he said. And then she had married him, telling him nothing of it, though she must have known that he would discover it as soon as she was his wife. It suited her to be his wife, — for some reason which he could not perceive. She had achieved her object; — but not on that account need he live with her. It had been an affair of money, and his money she might have.

He came back and got his horse, as the motion of walking was not fast enough for him in his passion. It was grievous to be borne, — the fact that he had been so mistaken in choosing for himself a special woman as a companion of his life. He had desired her to be all honour, all truth, all simplicity, and all innocence. And instead of these things he had encountered fraud and premeditated deceit. She was his wife indeed; — but not on that account need he live with her.

And then his curiosity was raised. What was the secret between them? There must have been some question of money, as to which at the last moment they had disagreed. To his thinking it was vile that a young woman should soil her mind with such thoughts and marry or reject a man at the last moment because of his money. All that should be arranged for her by her friends, so that she might go to her husband

151

without having been mixed in any question of a sordid matter. But these two had probably found at the last moment that their income was insufficient for their wants, and therefore his purse had been thought convenient. As all these things, with a thousand others, passed through his mind he came to the determination that at any rate they must part.

He came home, and before he ate his dinner he wrote to her that letter, of which the contents shall now be given. It was a most unreasonable letter. But to him in his sorrow, in his passion, it seemed that every word was based upon reason.

'DEAR CECILIA,' the letter ran,
'I need hardly tell you that I was surprised by the facts which you at last told me this morning. I should have been less pained, perhaps, had they come to me in the first instance from yourself instead of from Sir Francis Geraldine. But I do not know that the conclusion to which I have been forced would have been in any way altered had such been the case. I can hardly, I fear, make you understand the shock with which I have received the intelligence, that a month or two before I proposed to you you had been the promised wife of that man. I need hardly tell you that had I known that it was so I should not have offered you my hand. To say the least of it, I was led into my marriage by a mistake. But a marriage commenced with such a mistake as

that cannot be happy.

'As to your object I cannot surmise. But I suppose that you were satisfied, thinking me to be of a nature especially soft and gentle. But I fear I am not so. After what has passed I cannot bring myself to live with you again. Pray believe it. We have now parted for ever.

'As to your future welfare, and as to the honour which will be due to my name, which you must continue to bear, I am quite willing to make any arrangements which friends of yours shall think to be due to you. Half my income you shall have, and you shall live here in this house if it be thought well for you. In reference to these things your lawyers had better see my lawyers. In the meantime my bankers will cash your cheques. But believe me that I am gone, not to return.

'Your affectionate husband,
'GEORGE WESTERN.'

These words he wrote, struggling to be cool and rational while he wrote them, and then he departed, leaving the letter upon the table.

Chapter XIII

MRS WESTERN PREPARES TO LEAVE

Cecilia, when she first read her husband's letter, did not clearly understand it. It could not be that he intended to leave her for ever! They had been married but a few months, — a few months of inexpressible love and confidence; and it was impossible that he should intend that they should be thus parted. But when she had read it again and again, she began to perceive that it was so; 'Pray believe it. We have now parted for ever.' Had he stopped there her belief would have only been half-hearted. She would not in truth have thought that he had been in earnest in dooming her to eternal separation. But he had gone on with shocking coolness to tell her how he had arranged his plans for the future. 'Half my income you shall have.' 'You shall live here in this house, if it be thought well for you.' 'Your lawyer had better see my lawyer.' It was, in truth, his intention that it should be so. And she had already begun to have some knowledge of the persistency of his character. She was already aware that he was a man not likely to be moved from his word. He had gone, and it was his intention to go. And he had declared with a magnanimity which she now felt to be odious, and almost mean, what liberal arrangements he had made for her maintenance.

She was in no want of income. She told herself that she would rather starve in the street than eat his bread, unless she might eat it from the same loaf with him; that she would rather perish in the cold than enjoy the shelter of his roof, unless she might enjoy it with him.

There she remained the whole day by herself, thinking that something must occur to mitigate the severity of the sentence which he had pronounced against her. It could not be that he should leave her thus, — he whose every word, whose every tone, whose every look, whose every touch had hitherto been so full of tenderness. If he had loved as she had loved how could he live without her? He had explained his idea of a wife, and though he had spoken the words in his anger, still she had been proud. But now it seemed as though he would have her believe that she was wholly unnecessary to him. It could not be so. He could not so have deceived her. It must be that he would want her as she wanted him, and that he must return to her to satisfy the cravings of his own heart.

But as time went on her tenderness gradually turned to anger. He had pronounced the sentence, the heaviest sentence which his mind could invent against her whom he had made his own. Was that sentence just? She told herself again and again that it was most unjust. The fault which she had committed deserved no such punishment. She confessed to herself that she had promised to become the wife of a man unworthy of her; but when she had done so she had not known her present husband. He at least had no cause of anger with her in regard to that. And she, as soon as she had found out her mistake and the man's character had become in part revealed to her, had with a terrible courage taken the bull by the horns and broken away from the engagement which outward circumstances had made attractive. Then with her mother she had gone abroad, and there she had met with Mr Western. At the moment of their meeting she had been at any rate innocent in regard to him. From that moment she had performed her duty to him, and had been sincere in her love, even as such a man as Mr Western could desire, — with the one exception of her silence. It was true that she should have told him of Sir Francis Geraldine; — of her folly in accepting him and her courage in repudiating him. Day by day the days had gone by, and there had been some cause for fresh delay, that cause having ever reference to his immediate comfort. Did she not know that had she told him, his offer, his love, his marriage would have been the same? And now, was she to be turned adrift and thrown aside, rejected and got rid of at an instant's notice, because, for his comfort, the telling of her story had been delayed? The injustice, the cruelty, the inhumanity of such a punishment were very plain to her.

Could he do it? As her husband had he a right so to dismiss her from his bosom? And his money? Perish his money! And his house! The remembrance of the offers which he made to her aggravated her wrath bitterly. As his wife she had a right to his care, to his presence, and to his tenderness. She had not married him simply to be maintained and housed. Nor was that the meaning of their marriage contract. Before God he had no right to send her away from him, and to bid her live and die alone.

But though he had no right he had the power. She could not force him to be her companion. The law would give her only those things which she did not care to claim. He already offered more than the law would exact, and she despised his generosity. As long as he supported her the law could not bring him back and force him to give her to eat of his own loaf, and to drink of his own cup. The law would not oblige him to encircle her in his arms. The law would not compel him to let her rest upon his bosom. None of those privileges which were undoubtedly her own could the law obtain for her. He had said that he had gone, and would not return, and the law could not bring him back again. Then she sat and wept, and told herself how much better would have been that single life of which Miss Altifiorla had preached to her the advantages.

The second day since his departure had passed and she had taken no step. Alone she had given way to sorrow and to indignation, but as yet had decided on nothing. She had waited, still thinking that something would be done to soften her sorrow; but nothing had been done. The servants around her moved slowly, solemnly, and as though struck with awe. Her own maid had tried to say a word once and again, but had been silenced by the manner of her mistress. Cecilia, though she felt the weight of the silence, could not bring herself to tell the girl that her husband had left her for ever. The servants no doubt knew it all, but she could not bring herself to tell them that it was so. He had told her that her cheques on his bankers would be paid, but she had declared that on no account should any such cheque be drawn by her. If he had made up his mind to desert her and had already left her without intending further communication, she must provide for herself. She must go back to her mother, where the eyes of all Exeter would see her. But she must in the first instance write to her mother; and how could she explain to her mother all that had happened? Would even her own mother believe her when she said that she was already deserted by her husband for ever and ever because she had not told him the story respecting Sir Francis Geraldine?

On the third morning she resolved that she would write to her husband. It was not fit, so she told herself, that she should leave his house without some further word of instruction from him. But how to address him she was ignorant. He was gone, but she did not know whither. The servants, no doubt, knew where, but she could not bring herself to ask them. On the third day she wrote as follows. The reader will remember that that short scrawl which she addressed to him from her bedroom had not been sent.

'DEAR GEORGE, — This is the first letter I have written to you as your wife, and it will be very sad. I do not think that you can have remembered that yours would be the first which I had ever received from my husband. Your order has crushed me altogether. It shall, nevertheless, be obeyed as far as I am able to obey it. You say something as to your means, and something also as to your house. In that you cannot be obeyed. It is not possible that I should take your money or live in your house unless I am allowed to do so as your wife. The law, I think, says that I may do so. But the law, of course, cannot compel a man to be a loving, tender husband, or even to accept the tenderness of a loving wife. I know what you owe me, but I know also that I cannot exact it unless you can give it with all your heart. Your money and your house I will not have unless I can have them together with yourself. Your bread would choke me. Your roof would not shelter me. Your good things would be poison to me, — unless you were here to make me feel that they were yours also as well as mine. If you mean to insist on the severity of your order, you will have to get rid of me altogether. I shall then have come across two men of which I do not know whether to wonder most at the baseness of the one or the cruelty of the other. In that case I can only return to my mother. In that case you will not, I think, care much what may become of me; but as I shall still bear your name, it is, I suppose, proper that you should know where I purpose living.

'But, dear George, dearest George, — I wish you could know how much dearer to me in spite of your cruelty than all the world besides, — I cannot ever yet bring myself to believe that we can for ever be separated. Dear George, endeavour to think how small has been my offence and how tremendous is the punishment which you propose. The offence is so small that I will not let myself down by asking your pardon. Had you said a word sitting beside me, even a word of anger, then I could have done so. I think I could have made you believe how altogether accidental it had been. But I will not do so now. I should aggravate my own fault till it would appear to you that I had done something of which I ought to be ashamed, and which perhaps you ought not to forgive. I have done nothing of which I am ashamed, and nothing certainly which you ought even to think it necessary to pardon.'

When she had got so far she sat for a while thinking whether she would or would not tell him of the cause and the manner of her silence. Should she refer him to his sister, who understood so well how that silence had been produced? Should she explain to him that she had in the first case hesitated to tell him her story because her story had been so like to his own? But as she thought of it all, she declared to herself that were she to do so she would in truth condescend to ask his pardon. What she required of him was that he should acknowledge her nature, her character, her truth to be such that he had made a grievous mistake in attributing to her aught that was a just cause of anger. 'You stupid girl, you foolish girl, to have given yourself and me such cause for discomfort!' That he should have said to her, with his arm round her waist; — that and nothing more. Thinking of all this she resolved not to go into that subject. Should she ever do so it must be when he had come back to her, and was sitting with his arm around her waist. She ended her letter, therefore, very shortly.

'As I must wait here till I hear from you, and cannot even write to my mother till I do so, I must beg you to answer my letter quickly. I shall endeavour to go on without drawing any cheques. If I find it necessary I shall have to write to my mother for money.

'Your most affectionate wife,
'CECILIA WESTERN.'

'Oh, George, if you knew how I loved you!' Then, as she did not like to send the letter out among the servants without any address, and thus to confess to them that she did not know where her husband had gone, she directed the letter to his club in London.

During the next day or two the pity of her servants, the silent, unexpressed pity, was very hard to bear. As each morning came her punishment seemed to become more and more intolerable to her. She could not read. There were none among her friends, not even her mother, to whom she could write. It was still her hope, — her faintest hope, that she need confess to none of them the fact that her husband had quarrelled with her. She could only sit and ponder over the tyranny of the man who by his mere suspicions could subject a woman to so cruel a fate. But on the evening of the third day she was told that a gentleman had called to see her. Mr Graham sent his card in to her, and she at once recognised Mr Graham as her husband's attorney. She was sitting at the open window of her own bedroom, looking into the garden, and she was aware that she had been weeping! 'I will be down at once,' she said to the maid, 'if Mr Graham will wait.'

'Oh, ma'am, you do take on so dreadfully,' said the girl.

'Never mind, Mary. I will come down and see Mr Graham if you will leave me.'

'Oh, ma'am, oh, Miss Holt, I have known you so long, may I not say a word to you?'

'I am not Miss Holt. I am still entitled to bear my husband's name.' Then the girl, feeling herself to have been rebuked, was leaving the room, when her mistress jumped up from her seat, took her in her arms, and kissed her. 'Oh, Mary,' she said, 'I am unhappy, so unhappy! But pray do not tell them. It is true that you have known me long, and I can trust you.' Then the girl, crying much more bitterly than her mistress, left the room.

In a few minutes Cecilia followed her, and entered the parlour into which Mr Graham had been shown, without a sign of tears upon her cheeks. She had been able to assume a look of injured feminine dignity, of almost magnificent innocence, by which the lawyer was much startled. She was resolved at any rate to confess no injury done by herself to her husband, and to say nothing to Mr Graham of any injury done by him to her. Mr Graham, too, was a gentleman, a man over fifty years of age, who had been solicitor to Mr Western's father. He knew the husband in this case well, but he had as yet known nothing of the wife. He had been simply told by Mr Western to understand that he, Mr Western, had no fault to find with the lady; that he had not a word to say against her; but that unfortunately circumstances had so turned out that all married happiness was impossible for him. Mr Graham had endeavoured to learn the facts; but he had been aware that Mr Western was a man who would not bear to be cross-examined. A question or two he had asked, and had represented to his client how dreadful was the condition to which he was condemning both the lady and himself. But his observations were received with that peculiar cold civility which the man's manner assumed when he felt that interference was taken in matters which were essentially private to himself. 'It is so, Mr Graham, that in this case it cannot be avoided. I wish you to understand that all pecuniary arrangements are to be made for Mrs Western which she herself may desire. Were she to ask for everything I possess she must have it, — down to the barest pittance.' But at this moment he had not received his wife's letter.

There was a majesty of beauty about Mrs Western by which Mr Graham was startled, but which he came to recognise before the interview was over. I cannot say that he understood the cause of the quarrel, but he had become aware that there was much in the lady very much on a par with her husband's character. And she, when she found out, as she did instinctively, that she had to deal with a gentleman, dropped something of the hauteur of her silence. But she said not a word as to the cause of their disagreement. Mr Graham asked the question in the simplest language. 'Can you not tell me why you two have quarrelled so quickly after your marriage?' But she simply referred him to her husband. 'I think you must ask Mr Western about that.' Mr Graham renewed the question, feeling how important it was that he should know. But she only smiled, and again referred him to her husband.

164

But when he came to speak to her about money arrangements she smiled no longer. 'It will not be necessary,' she said.

'But it is Mr Western's wish.'

'It will not be necessary. Mr Western has decided that we must — part. On that matter I have not a word to say. But there will be nothing for any lawyer to do on my behalf. If Mr Western has made up his mind, I will return to my mother. I can assure you that no steps need be taken as to money. 'No steps will be possible,' she added, with all that feminine majesty which was peculiar to her. 'I understand from you that Mr Western's mind is made up. You can tell him that I shall be ready to leave this house for my mother's, in — let me say a week.' Mr Graham went back to town having been able to make no other arrangement. He might pay the servant's wages, — when they were due; and the tradesmen's bills; but for herself and her own peculiar wants Mrs Western would take no money. 'You may tell Mr Western,' she said, 'that I shall not have to encroach on his liberality.' So Mr Graham went back to town; and Mrs Western carried herself through the interview without the shedding of a tear, without the utterance of a word of tenderness, — so that the lawyer on leaving her hardly knew what her wishes were.

'Nevertheless I think it is his doing,' he said to himself. 'I think she loves him.'

Chapter XIV

TO WHAT A PUNISHMENT!

Mr Western, when he received his wife's letter, after having given his instructions to the lawyer, was miserable enough. But not on that account did he think of changing his purpose. He had made up his mind, — as men say, — and having made it up he assured himself that he had done it with ample cause. He could not quite explain to himself the reasons for his anger. He did not quite know what were the faults of which he accused his wife. But he was sure that his wrath was just, and had come from sins on her part which it would be unbecoming as a man and a husband that he should condone. And his anger was the hotter because he did not know what those sins were. There had been some understanding, — so he thought, — between his wife and Sir Francis Geraldine which was derogatory to his honour. There had been an understanding and a subsequent quarrel, and Sir Francis Geraldine had been base enough to inform him of the understanding because of the quarrel. Sir Francis no doubt had been very base, but not on that account had his wife been less a sinner. What was it to him that Sir Francis should be base? No vice, no lies, no cruelty on the part of Sir Francis were anything to him. But his wife; — that she whom he had taken to his bosom as his own, that she in whom he had believed, she who was to be the future depository of all his secrets, his very second self, that she, in the very moment in which he had exposed to her the tenderness of his heart, that she should then have entertained a confidential intercourse with such a one as Sir Francis Geraldine, an intercourse of which she had intended that he should know nothing, — that, that was more than he could endure. It was this — this feeling that he was to know nothing of it, which was too much for him. It seemed to him that he had been selected to be a stalking-horse for them in their intercourse. It was not that he ever accused his wife of illicit love. He was not base enough to think her so base as that. But there had been some cause for a mysterious alliance as to which he had been kept in the dark. To be kept in the dark, and by his own wife, was the one thing that was unendurable. And then the light had been let in upon him by that letter from Sir Francis, in which Sir Francis had offered 'such courtesies as are generally held to be pleasant in a neighbourhood'! The intention had been that this old friendship should be renewed under his roof, and be renewed without any information being given to him that it had ever previously existed. This was the feeling that had made it incumbent on him to repudiate a wife who had so treated him. This was the feeling which forbad him to retire from his suicidal purpose. His wife had had a secret, a secret which it was not intended that he should share, and her partner in the secret had been that man whom of all men he had despised the most, and who as he now learnt had been only the other day engaged to marry her. In fostering his wrath he had declared to himself that it was but only the other day; and he had come to think that at the very moment in which he had told Cecilia Holt of all his own troubles she had then, even then, been engaged to this abominable baronet. 'I have got another man to offer to marry me, and therefore our engagement, which is a trouble to us both, may now be over.' Some such communication as this had been made, and he had been the victim of it.

And yet as he thought of all this, and nursed his rage, and told himself how impossible it was that he should even pretend to live with such a woman with continued confidence, even then he was at moments almost overcome by the tenderness of his recollections. He had loved her so entirely; and she to his outward eyes and outward ears been so fit to be loved! He had thanked his stars that after running into so great a peril with that other lady it had at last been given to him to settle his heart where it might dwell securely. She had required from him no compliments, none of the little weaknesses of love-making, no pretences, had demanded from him the taking of no trouble which would have grated against his feeling. She had been everything that his very soul desired. And she had played her part so well! She had been to him as though it had been a fresh thing to her to love a man with all her heart, and to be able to talk to him of her love. And yet she, the while, was in secret and most intimate communication with a man to whom he had been in the habit of applying within his own breast all the vilest epithets which the language could afford. 'Swindler, thief, scoundrel', were the terms he had thought of. In his dislike to the ways of the world in general he had declared to himself that the world admitted such as Sir Francis within its high places without disgust. This was the man who had coolly demanded to be intimate with him, and had done so in order that he might maintain his acquaintance with his wife!

We know how wrong he was in these thoughts; — how grievously he wronged her of whom he was thinking. Of the worst of all these sins she was absolutely innocent; — of so much the worst that the fault of which she had not been innocent was not worth regarding when thought of in reference to that other crime. But still it was thus that he believed, and though he was aware that he was about to submit himself to absolute misery in decreeing their separation, yet there was to his thinking no other remedy. He had been kept in the dark. To the secrets of others around him he was, he declared to himself, absolutely indifferent. They might have their mysteries and it would be nothing to him. He had desired to have one whose mysteries should be his mysteries; who should share every thought of his heart, and of whose secret thoughts he desired to keep the only key. He had flattered himself that it was so, and this had been the result! It may be doubted whether his misery were not altogether as bitter as hers. 'Of course she shall live with her mother if she pleases it,' he said to Mr Graham on the following morning. 'As to money, if she will name no sum that she requires I must leave it to you to say what in justice ought to be allowed to her. You know all the circumstances of my property.'

'But I know none of the circumstances of your marriage,' replied Mr Graham.

'They were altogether of the usual kind.'

'None of the circumstances of your separation, I should have said.'

'It is unnecessary,' replied Mr Western, gloomily.

'It will be very difficult to give her any advice.'

'You may take it if you will that the fault is all mine. I would provide for her as I should be bound to do if by my own cruelty or my own misconduct I had driven her from me!' He had no idea as he said this that by his own cruelty and his own misconduct he was driving her from him.

'My conviction is that she will take nothing,' said Mr Graham.

'In a matter of business she must take it. The money must be paid to her, let her do what she will with it. Even though it should be thrown into the sea, I must pay it.'

'I think you will find that she has a will of her own.' 'And she will find that I have,' said Mr Western with a frown. It was exactly on this point that the husband and wife were being separated. He had thought that she had calculated that when once they were married she had carried her purpose in spite of his will. But he would let her understand that it was not so. She had so far succeeded that she was entitled to bear his name, but she had not mastered him in the matter, and should not do so.

'It is a thousand pities, Mr Western. You will allow me to say so, but it is a thousand pities. A most handsome lady; — with a fine lady-like air! One in a thousand!'

Mr Western could not endure to hear the catalogue of his wife's charms set forth to him. He did not want to be told by his lawyer that she was 'handsome' and 'one in a thousand!' In that respect their quarrel made no difference. No gentleman wishes another to assure him that his wife is one in a thousand. An old mother might say so, or an old aunt; hardly any one less near and less intimate could be allowed to do so. Mr Western was aware that no man in the ordinary course of events would be less likely to offend in that way than Mr Graham. But in this case Mr Graham should not, he thought, have done it. He had come to Mr Graham about money and not about his wife's beauty. 'I hardly think we need discuss that,' he said, still with a heavy frown on his brow. 'Perhaps you will think over what I have said to you, and name a sum to-morrow.'

'At the risk of making you angry I have to speak,' continued Mr Graham. 'I knew your father, and have known you all your life. If this is to make her miserable, and if, as I gather, she has committed no great fault, will it not be — wicked?' Mr Graham sat silent for a few moments, looking him in the face. 'Have you consulted your own conscience, and what it will say to you after a time? She has given all that she has to you, though there has not been a shilling, — and no money can repay her. One fault is not pardonable, — one only fault.'

'No, no. I do not accuse her.'

'Nor dream that she is guilty, — if I understand the matter rightly.'

'No, I do not. But I did not come here to be interrogated about her after this fashion, — nor to be told that I am wicked. For what sins I commit I must be myself responsible. I am unable, — at any rate unwilling, — to tell you the circumstances, and must leave you to draw your own conclusions. If you will think over the matter, and will name a sum, I shall be obliged to you.' Then he was about to leave, but Mr Graham interposed himself between his client and the door.

'Pray excuse me, Mr Western. I know that you are angry, but pray excuse me. I should ill do my duty to an old client whom I respect did I not dare, as being older than he is, to give the advice

which as a bystander I think that he requires.'
Mr Western stood perfectly silent before him but
clearly showing his wrath by the frown upon his
brow. 'I venture to say that you are taking upon
yourself as a husband to do that which the world
will not pardon.'

'I care nothing for the world.'

'Pardon me. You will care for it when you
come to consider that its decision has been just.
When you have to reflect that you have ruined
for ever the happiness of a woman whom you
have sworn to love and protect, and that you
have cast her from you for some reason which
you cannot declare and which is not held to justify such usage, then you will regard what the
world says. You will regard it because your own
conscience will say the same. If I mistake not you
still love her.'

'I am not here to discuss such points,' said Mr
Western angrily.

'Think of the severity of the punishment
which you are inflicting upon one whom you
love; and of the effect it must have on her feelings. I tell you that you have no right to do this,
— unless she have been guilty, as you confess she
has not.' Then he seated himself in his arm-chair
and Mr Western left the chamber without saying
another word.

He went out into Lincoln's Inn, and walked
westward towards his Club, hardly knowing in
his confusion whither he was going. At first his
breast was hot with anger against Mr Graham.

The man had called him wicked and cruel, and had known nothing of the circumstances. Could it be wicked, could it be cruel for him to resent such treachery as that of which he had been the victim? All his holiest hopes had been used against him for the vilest purposes and with the most fell effect! He at any rate had been ruined for ever. And the man had told him about the world! What did he in his misery care for the world's judgment? Cecilia had married him, — and in marrying him had torn his heart asunder. This man had accused him of cruelty in leaving her. But how could he have continued to live with her without hypocrisy? Cruel indeed! What were her sufferings to his — hers, who had condescended to the level of Sir Francis Geraldine, and had trafficked with such a one as that as to the affairs of their joint happiness! To such a woman it was not given to suffer. Yes; she was beautiful and she looked as a lady should look. Mr Graham had been right enough in that. But he had not known how looks may deceive, how noble to the eye may be the face of a woman while her heart within is ignoble, paltry, and mean. But as he went on with his walk by degrees he came to forget Mr Graham, and to think of the misery which was in store for himself. And though at the moment he despised Mr Graham, his thoughts did occupy themselves exactly with those perils of which Mr Graham had spoken. The woman had trusted herself to his care and had given him her beauty and her solicitude. He did in his heart believe that she loved him. He remembered the last words of her letter — 'Oh George, if you knew how I loved you!' He did not doubt but that those words were true. He did not suppose that she had ever given her heart to Sir Francis Geraldine, — that she had truly and sincerely devoted herself to one so mean as that! Such heart as she had to give had been given to himself. But there had been traffic of marriage with this man, and even continued correspondence and an understanding as to things which had put her with all her loveliness on a level with him rather than with her existing husband. What this understanding was he did not he said care to inquire. It had existed and still did exist. That was enough to make him know that she was untrue to him as his wife, — untrue in spirit if not in body. But in truth he did care to know. It was, indeed, because he had not known, because he had been allowed only to guess and search and think about it, that all this misery had come. He had been kept in the dark, and to be kept in the dark was to him, of all troubles, the most grievous. When he had first received the letter from Sir Francis he had not believed it to be true. From first to last it had been a fiction. But when once his wife had told him that the engagement had existed, he believed all. It was as though she had owned to him the circumstance of a still existing intimate friendship. He had been kept in the dark, but he did not know how far.

But still there loomed to him as to the future,

vaguely, the idea that by the deed he was doing now, at this present moment, he was sacrificing her happiness and his own for ever, — as regarded this world. And the people would say that he had done so, — the people whose voices he could not but regard. She would say so, and her mother, — and he must acknowledge it. And Lady Grant would know that it had been so, and Mr Graham would always think so to the end. And his heart became tender even towards her. What would be her fate, — as his wife and therefore debarred from the prospects of any other future? She would live with her mother as any widow would live, — with much less of hope, with less chance of enjoying her life, than would any other widow. And when her mother should die she would be all alone. To what a punishment was he not dooming her!

If he could die himself it would be well for all parties. He had taken his great step in life and had failed. Why should he doom her who was differently constituted, to similar failure? It had been a great mistake. He had made it and now there was no escape. But then again his pity for himself welled up in his heart. Why had he been so allured, so deceived, so cozened? He had intended to have given all good things. The very essence of his own being he had bestowed upon her, — while she, the moment that his back was turned, was corresponding with Sir Francis Geraldine! That thought he could not stand. She, in truth, had been greatly in error in her first view of the character of Sir Francis Geraldine; but it must be a question whether he was not so also. The baronet was a poor creature; but not probably so utterly vile as he thought him. As he turned it all over in his mind, while wandering to and fro, he came to the conclusion that Mr Graham was wrong, and that it was impossible that she, who had been the sharer of the thoughts of Sir Francis Geraldine, should now remain to share his.

Chapter XV

ONCE MORE
AT EXETER

Three weeks had passed and much had been done for Mrs Western to fix her fate in life. It was now August, and she was already living at Exeter as a wife separated from her husband. Of much she had had to think and much to determine before she had found that haven of rest. Twice during the time she had received letters from her husband, but each letter had been short, and, though not absolutely without affection in its language, each letter had been absolutely obdurate. He had been made quite sure that it was not for the benefit of either of them that they should attempt to live together. Having come to that decision, which he represented as unchangeable, he was willing, he said, to do anything which she might demand for her future satisfaction and comfort. 'There is nothing you can do,' she had said when she had written last, 'as you have refused to do your duty.' This had made him again angry. 'What right has she to talk to me of my duty, seeing that she has so grossly neglected her own?' he said to himself. Then he had suddenly gone from England, leaving no address even with his sister or with his lawyer. But during this time his mind was not quiet for one instant. How could she have treated him so, him, who had been so absolutely devoted to her, who had so entirely given himself up to her happiness?

Lady Grant, when she had heard what was to be done, had hurried up to London but had not found them. She had gone to Exeter and there she had in vain endeavoured to comfort Cecilia. She had declared that her brother would in time forgive. But Cecilia's whole nature had by this time apparently been changed. 'Forgive!' she had said. 'What will he forgive? There is nothing that he can forgive; nothing that can be spoken of in the same breath with his perfidy and cruelty. Can I forgive? Ask yourself that, Lady Grant. Is it possible that I should forgive?' After two days spent in conversations such as these Lady Grant went back to town and discussed the matter with Mr Graham. They did not at present know her brother's address; but still there was a hope that she might induce him to hear reason and again to consent to live with his wife. 'Of all men,' she said to the lawyer, 'he is the most honest and the most affectionate; but of all men the most self-willed and obstinate. An injustice is with him like a running sore; and, alas, it is not always an injustice, but a something that he has believed to be unjust.'

Cecilia had written at great length to her mother, telling her with all details the story as it was to be told, and sparing herself in nothing. 'That wicked man has contrived it all. But, oh, that such a one as my husband should have been weak enough to have fallen into a pit so prepared!' Then Mrs Holt had come up to town and taken her daughter back with her to Exeter. Now, at last, on this occasion, the old woman was both energetic and passionate. There had been much discussion before they had both decided, that they would again venture to live together among their old friends in their old home. But here Cecilia had shown herself to be once again stronger than her mother. 'Why not?' she said. 'What have I done to make it necessary that you should be torn away from your house? I am not at all ashamed of what I have done.' In this she had blazoned forth her courage with almost a false conviction. She knew that she had done wrong; — that she had done that of which among wives she ought to be ashamed. But her sin had been so small in comparison with the punishment inflicted upon her that it sunk to nothing even in her own eyes. She felt that she had been barbarously used. The people of Exeter, or the people of the world at large, might sympathise with her or not as they pleased. But under such a mountain of wrong as she had endured, she would not show by any conduct of her own that she could have in the least deserved it. 'No, mamma,' she said; 'let them stay away or let them come, I shall be ready for either. I am a poor wretched woman, whom to crush utterly has been within the power of the man she has loved. He has chosen to exercise it and I must suffer. But he shall not make me ashamed. I have done nothing to deserve his cruelty.'

And then when she had been at Exeter but a few days there came another source of trouble, — though not of unmitigated trouble. She told her mother that in due course of time her cruel husband would become the father of a child. She would not write to him. He had not chosen to let her know his address; nor was it fitting to her feelings to communicate such a fact in a letter which she must address secretly to his banker or to his club. Yet the fact was of such a nature that it was imperative that he should know it. At last it was told by Mrs Holt to Lady Grant. Cecilia had herself attempted it, but had found that she could not do it. She could not write the letter without some word of tenderness, and she was resolved that no word of tenderness should go from her to him. It would seem as though she were asking for money, and were putting forward the coming of the little stranger as a plea for it. She would ask for no money. She had appealed to his love, and had appealed in vain. If he were hard, she would be so too. In her heart of hearts she probably entertained the idea of some possible future in which she might yet put the child into its father's arms; — but it should be done not at her request. It should be at his prayer. At least there was this comfort to her, — that she no longer dreaded his power. He had so contrived that to her thinking the fault was altogether on his side. Forgive! Oh yes; she would forgive! Oh yes; she would forgive, so readily, so sweetly, with the full determination that it should all be like a black nightmare that had come between them and troubled their joys. But in the bottom of the heart of each it must be understood that it had been hers to pardon and his to be pardoned. Or if not so, then she must continue to live her widowed life at Exeter.

Mrs Holt was energetic and passionate rather than discreet. She would not admit that her child had done any wrong, and could not be got to understand but that the law should make a husband live with his wife in the proper way. It was monstrous to her thinking that her daughter should be married and taken away, and then sent back, without any offence on her part. In the resentment which she felt against Mr Western she filled quite a new part among the people of Exeter. 'Oh, mamma; you are so loving, so good,' said her daughter; 'but do not let us talk about it. Cannot you understand that, angry as I am, I cannot endure to have him abused?' 'Abused!' said Mrs Holt, kindling in her wrath. 'I cannot hold myself without abusing him.' But it very soon did come to pass that Mr Western's name was not mentioned between them. Mrs Holt would now and again clench her fist and shake her head, and Cecilia knew that in her thoughts she was executing some vengeance against Mr Western; but there was a truce to spoken words. Cecilia indeed often executed her vengeance against her husband after some fashion of her own, but her mother did not perceive it.

Among their Exeter friends there soon came to

be an actual breach with Miss Altifiorla. Miss Altifiorla, as soon as it was known that Mrs Western had reappeared in Exeter, had rushed down to greet her friend. There she had been received coldly by Cecilia, and more than coldly by Cecilia's mother. 'My dear Cecilia,' she had said, attempting to take hold of her friend's hand, 'I told you what would come of it.'

'There need be nothing said about it,' said Mrs Western.

'Not after the first occasion,' said Miss Altifiorla. 'A few words between us to show that each understands the other will be expedient.'

'I do not see that any words can be of service,' said Mrs Western. 'Not in the least,' said Mrs Holt. 'Why need anything be said? You know that she has been cruelly ill-used, and that is all you need know.'

'I do know the whole history of it,' said Miss Altifiorla, who had taken great pride to herself among the people of Exeter in being the best informed person there as to Mrs Western's sad affairs. 'I was present up to the moment, and I must say that if Cecilia had then taken my advice things would have been very different. I am not blaming her.'

'I should hope not,' said Mrs Holt.

'But things would have been very different. Cecilia was a little timid at telling her husband the truth. And Mr Western was like other gentlemen. He did not like to be kept in the dark by his wife. You see that Cecilia has given mortal cause for offence to two gentlemen.'

This was not to be endured. Cecilia did not exactly know all the facts as they had occurred, — between Miss Altifiorla and Sir Francis, — and certainly knew none of those which were now in process of occurring; but she strongly suspected that something had taken place, that some conversation had been held, between her friend and Sir Francis Geraldine. She had been allowed to read the letter from Sir Francis to her husband, and she remembered well the meaning of it. But she could not remember the terms which he had used. She had, however, thought that something which had passed between himself and Miss Altifiorla had been the immediate cause of the writing of that letter. She did think that Miss Altifiorla had, as it were, gone over to the enemy. That she had been prepared to pardon. The enemy had, in fact, told no falsehood in his letter. It had been her misfortune that the story which he had told had been true; — and her further misfortune that her husband should have believed so much more than the truth. For all that she did not hold Miss Altifiorla to be responsible. But when she was told that she had given cause for mortal offence to two gentlemen, there was something in the phrase which greatly aggravated her anger. It was as though this would-be friend was turning against her for her conduct towards Sir Francis. And she was just as angry that the friend should turn against her for her conduct to her husband. 'Miss Altifiorla,' she said, 'I must request that there be no further conversation between us in reference to the difference between me and my husband.'

'Miss Altifiorla! Is it to come to that, Cecilia — between you and me who have enjoyed so much sweet friendship?'

'Certainly; if you make yourself so offensive,' said Mrs Holt.

'It is the only mode by which I can show that I am in earnest,' said Cecilia. 'If it does not succeed, I must declare that I shall be unwilling to meet you at all. I told you to be silent, and you would not.'

'Oh, very well! If you like to quarrel it will quite suit me. But in your present condition I hardly think that you are wise in throwing off your old friends. It is just the time when you ought to cling to those who would be true to you.'

This was more than Cecilia could bear. 'I shall cling to those who are true to me,' she said, leaving the room.

'Oh, very well! Then I shall know how to conduct myself.' This was addressed to Mrs Holt. 'I hope you will conduct yourself, as you call it, somewhere away from here. You're very fond of meddling, that's the truth; and Cecilia in her present condition does not want to be meddled with. Oh, yes, you can go away as soon as ever you please!' Thereupon Miss Altifiorla left the room and withdrew. It must be explained that this lady, since she was last upon the scene, had learned to entertain new hopes, very exalted in their nature. It had first occurred to her during those ten minutes at the Paddington railway station, that it might possibly be so if she played her cards well. And then how glorious would be the result! Sir Francis Geraldine had squeezed her hand. If he might be made to go on squeezing her hand sufficiently, how great might be the effect produced! Lady Geraldine! How beautiful was the sound! She thought that within all the bounds of the English peerage, — and she knew that those bounds included the baronets, — there was no sweeter, no more glorious, no more aristocratic appellation. Lady Geraldine! What a change, what a blissful change would that be! When she thought of the chill of her present life, of its want of interest, of its insipid loneliness, and then told herself what might be in store for her should she live to become Lady Geraldine, she declared to herself that even though the chance might be very small, the greatness of the reward if gained would justify the effort. Lady Geraldine! And she saw no reason why her chance should be so very small. She had a cousin with a pedigree longer than even that of Sir Francis, Count Altifiorla, — who, indeed, had no money, but was a genuine Count. She herself had a nice little sum of money, quite enough to be agreeable to a gentleman who might be somewhat out of elbows from the effects of Newmarket. And she did not think too little of her own personal appearance. She knew that she had a good wearing complexion and that her features were of that sort which did not yield very readily to the hand of time. There were none of the endearing dimples of early youth, none of the special brightness of English feminine loveliness, none of the fresh tints of sweet girlhood; but Miss Altifiorla boasted to herself that she would look the British aristocratic matron very well. She certainly had not that Juno beauty which Cecilia Holt could boast, that beauty which could be so severe to all chance comers but which could melt at once and become soft and sweet and easy to one favoured individual. Miss Altifiorla acknowledged to herself that it was her nature always to remain outwardly the same to all men. But then dress and diamonds, and all the applied paraphernalia of aristocracy would, she felt, go far with her. If Sir Francis could be once got to admire her, she was sure that Sir Francis would never be driven to repent of his bargain from any falling off on her part. She thought that she would know how to be the master; but this would be an after consideration, and one as to which she need not at present pay especial attention. Sir Francis had squeezed her hand most affectionately, and there had been a subsequent meeting at Exeter, where he had stayed a couple of hours as he went through to his own property. And she was sure that he had stayed for the purpose of meeting her. Since that affair with Cecilia Holt he had not been made warmly welcome at the Deanery. Yet he had stayed and had absolutely called upon Miss Altifiorla. He had found her and had discussed Mr and Mrs Western with much sarcastic humour.

'Now you haven't!' Miss Altifiorla had said, when he told her of the letter he had written. 'How could you be so hard upon the poor man?' 'Perhaps the lady may think that I have been hard upon her,' Sir Francis had replied. 'Perhaps she will know the meaning of tit for tat. Perhaps she will understand now that one good turn deserves another. It was not that I cared so much for her,' he said. 'I'd got to feel that she was far too virtuous for me, — too stuck up, you'll understand. I wasn't at all disappointed when she played me that trick. She didn't turn out the sort of girl that I had taken her for. I knew that I had had an escape. But, nevertheless, tit for tat is fair on both sides. She played me a trick, and now I've played her one, and we are even. We can each go to work again. She began a little too soon, perhaps, for her own comfort; but that's her affair, not mine.'

In answer to all this, Miss Altifiorla had only laughed and smiled and declared that Cecilia had been served right, though she thought, — she said that she thought, — that Sir Francis had been almost too hard. 'That's my way of doing business,' he had added. 'If any one wants me to run straight, they must begin by running straight themselves. I can be as sweet as new milk if I'm well treated.' Then there had been a moment in which Miss Altifiorla had almost expected that he was going to do something preparatory to declaring himself. She was convinced that he was about to kiss her; but at the very moment at which the event had been expected, Mrs Green had been announced and the kiss did not, alas! come off. She could hardly bring herself to be civil to Mrs Green when Sir Francis declared that he must go to the station.

Chapter XVI

'IT IS ALTOGETHER UNTRUE.'

The month of September wore itself away at Exeter very sadly. An attempt was made to bid Mrs Western welcome back to her old home; but from the nature of the circumstances there could hardly be much heartiness in the attempt. Mrs Thorne came over from Honiton to see her, but even between Cecilia and Maude Hippesley, who was certainly the most cherished of her Exeter friends, there could be no free confidence, although there was much sympathy. Mrs Western could bring herself to speak evil to no one of her husband. She had, with much passion, told the entire story to her mother, but when her mother had begun to say hard words respecting him Cecilia had found it impossible to bear them. Had her mother taken Mr Western's part, it may be doubted whether she could have endured that. There was no speech concerning him which was possible for her ears. She still looked forward to the chance of having him back again, and if he would come back, if he would take her back, then he should be entirely forgiven. He should be so forgiven that no mutual friend should have heard a word of reproach from her lips. She herself would know how hardly she had been used; but there should be no one to say that she had ever been heard to complain of her husband. Not the less was her heart full of wrath. Not the less did she during every hour of the day turn over in her thoughts the terrible injustice of which she had been the victim. But it can be understood that even to her old friend Maude Hippesley, who was now happy in her new home as Mrs Thorne, she could not talk openly of the circumstances of her separation. But there was, alas, no other subject of such interest to her at the present moment as to give matter for free conversation.

The Dean's family, and especially Mrs Hippesley, attempted to be kind to her. The Dean himself came down and called with much decanal grandeur, conspicuous as he walked up to the Hall door with shovel hat and knee breeches. But even the Dean could not do much. He had intended to take Mrs Western's part as against his brother-in-law, having been no doubt prompted by some old feeling of favour towards Cecilia Holt; but now he was given to understand that this Mr Western had also gone astray, and in such a way as to make it hardly possible that he should talk about it. He called therefore and took her by the hand, and expressed a hope that all things should be made to go straight, and then he left her, taking her by the hand again, and endeavouring to prove his esteem by his manner of doing so. That was the beginning and the end of the Dean's comforting. Mrs Hippesley could do but little more. She did make an attempt at confidential conversation, but was soon stopped by Cecilia's cold manner. Mrs Western, indeed, could speak to none. She could not utter a word either for or against her husband. Mrs Green came, of course, more than once; but it was the same thing. Mrs Western could endure to talk and to be talked to about nothing. And though there was friendship in it, it was but a subdued feeling of friendship, — of friendship which under the circumstances had to be made silent. Mrs Green when she had taken her leave determined not to come again immediately, and Mrs Western when Mrs Green had gone felt that she did not wish her to come. She could live with her mother more easily than with her old friends, because her mother understood the tone of her mind. Each kept their thoughts to themselves on that subject of which each was thinking; but each sympathised with the other.

Lady Grant as soon as she understood the condition of things at once began to correspond with her brother. To her it was a matter of course that he should, sooner or later, take his wife back again. But to her thinking it was most important that he should do so before the fact of their quarrel had been flaunted before the world by an enduring separation. She wrote in the first instance without throwing blame upon either party, but calling upon her brother to show the honesty and honour of his purpose by coming back at once to Durton Lodge, and receiving Cecilia. 'Of course it must be so sooner or later,' said Lady Grant, 'and the quicker you do it so much easier will be the doing.' It should be told that Mrs Holt had, without telling her daughter, in her passion, herself written to Mr Western. 'You have sacrificed my daughter in your perversity, and that without the slightest cause for blame.' Such had been the nature of Mrs Holt's letter, which had reached him but a day before that of his sister. Lady Grant's appeal had not been of the same nature. She had said nothing of the sin of either of them; but had written as though both had been in fault, misunderstanding each other, and neither having been willing to yield a little. Then she had appealed to her brother's love and affectionate disposition. It was not till afterwards that she had been able to inform him of the baby that was expected.

Mr Western answered his sister's letter from Dresden. To Mrs Holt he sent no reply; but he used her letter as the ground for that which he made to Lady Grant, writing as though Mrs Holt's words had come directly from his wife. 'They say that I have sacrificed Cecilia without the slightest fault on her part. I have not sacrificed her, and there has been terrible fault on her part. Fault! A young woman marries a man while she is yet engaged to another, and tells the poor dupe whom she has got within her clutches nothing of her first engagement! Is there no fault in that? And she afterwards entertains the first man at her husband's house, and corresponds with him, and prepares at last to receive him there as a friend, and that without a word on the subject spoken to her husband! Is there no fault in that? And at last the truth becomes known to him because the base man is discontented with the arrangements that have been made, and chooses to punish her by exposing her at last to the wrath of her husband! I say nothing of him. With his conduct in the world I have no concern. But can all that have taken place with no fault on her part? What in such a state of things should I have done? Should I have contented myself simply with forbidding my wife to receive the man at my house? Should I have asked her no question as to the past? Should I have passed over that engagement which had been in full existence during the last twelve months, and have said nothing of it? Or should I have expressed my anger and then have forgiven her and attempted to live with her as though this man had never existed? Knowing me as you do, can you say that that would have been possible to me? How could I have lived with a wife of whom I knew so much as I had then learned of mine, — but had known so little before? Had I been a man of the world, living for the world, careless as to my own home except as to the excellence of my dinner and the comfort of my bed, it might have been possible. A man trusting for his happiness to such means might perhaps have continued to exist and not have been broken-hearted. But I think you will understand that such could not be the case with me. I looked for my happiness to my wife's society and I discovered when I had married that I could not find it there. I could never respect her!

'But she tells me that having married her I have no right to sacrifice her. As I had been fool enough to allow myself to be so quickly allured by her charms, and had made those charms my own, I was bound to stand by my bargain! That I take it is the argument which her mother uses. I grant the truth of it. It is I that should be sacrificed and not she. I have so acted that I am bound to submit myself to such a verdict. What the law would require from me I cannot say. The law might perhaps demand a third of my income. She shall have two-thirds if she wishes it. She shall have seven-eighths if she will ask for it. At present I have given instructions by which during her life she shall have one half. I am aware that in the heat of her passion she has declined to accept this. It shall nevertheless be paid to her credit. And I must deny that one who has achieved her marriage after such a fashion has any right, when so treated, to regard herself as sacrificed. I am the victim. But as I am convinced that she and I cannot live happily together, I reserve to myself the right of living apart.'

Lady Grant, when she received this letter, immediately sat down to write to Cecilia, but she soon found it to be impossible to put into a letter all that there was to be said. She was living in the neighbourhood of Perth whereas her sister-in-law was at Exeter. And yet the matter was of such moment that she perceived it to be essential that they should see each other. Perhaps it might be better that Mrs Western should come to her; and therefore she wrote to her, — not explaining the cause of the proposed visit, to do which would be as difficult as to write the full letter, but simply saying that in the present condition of things she thought it would be well that Cecilia should visit her. This however Mrs Western refused to do. She had come to her mother, she said, in her terrible difficulty, and in her present circumstances would not at once leave her. She considered herself bound to obey her husband, and would remain at Exeter until she received instructions from him to leave it.

There was in her letter a subdued tone of displeasure, which Lady Grant felt that she had not deserved. She at any rate was anxious to do her best. But she would not on that account abandon the task which she had undertaken. Her only doubt was whether she had better go to her brother at Berlin or to his wife at Exeter. She understood perfectly now the nature of those mistaken suspicions which filled her brother's mind. And she was almost sure of the circumstances which had produced them. But she was not quite sure; and were she to make mistakes in discussing the matter with him, such mistakes might be fatal. She thought that with Cecilia she could not do other than good. She knew her brother's mind better than did his wife, and she imagined that between them such a story might be told, — a story so true and so convincing that the husband might be brought back.

The following very short letter therefore was written.

'MY DEAR CECILIA, as you will not come to me at Perth, I must go to you at Exeter. I shall start this day week and will be with you on the following Wednesday. Do not mind as to a room for me, as I can stop at the hotel; but it is I think imperative that we should see each other.

Yours affectionately,
BERTHA GRANT.'

'Mamma, Lady Grant is coming here next week,' said Cecilia to her mother.

'To this house, next week?'

'She says that she will come to the hotel; but of course we must receive her here.'

'But why is she coming?'

'I suppose it is because she thinks that something should be done on behalf of her brother. I can understand her feeling, and am sure that she sympathises with me. But I do not think that any good will come of it. Unless he can see how wrong he is nothing will be able to change him. And until his very nature is changed he will not be made to understand his own fault.' It was thus for the first time for a fortnight that Mrs Western spoke to her mother about her husband.

At the day appointed Lady Grant came and

Mrs Western met her at the station. 'Of course you will not go to the hotel,' she said; 'there is plenty of room at the house. I am greatly obliged to you for coming. It seems a dreadful thing to have to come on such a business all the way from Perth. I know that I ought to apologise to you for the trouble.'

'Apologise! There can be no apologising between you and me. If I can make each of you understand the truth there is not I think any doubt but that you will be brought together.'

'If he can be made to see the truth, it may be so. I do not know that there is any seeing of the truth necessary on the other side. I have complained of nothing. He has taken upon himself to leave me for some cause as to which I am perfectly in the dark. However we will not talk about it now.' Then she put Lady Grant into the fly and took her home.

There was nothing more said about it on that day. Mrs Western, in whose bosom something of her feeling of anger against her husband was most unjustly extended towards Lady Grant, took care that they two should not be at once left together again. Mrs Holt was studiously civil, but always with a feeling that Mr Western and Lady Grant were brother and sister. It was probable that the sister would take her brother's part and consequently be at any moment converted into an enemy. The first evening at Exeter was passed very uncomfortably by the three ladies. But on the following morning a conference was demanded. 'My dear,' said Lady Grant, 'we have got to discuss all this and we may as well do it at once. What does your husband mean when he says that you were still engaged to Sir Francis when you became engaged to him?'

'Has he said so?'

'Yes; indeed.'

'Then he has said what is altogether untrue. Nor is there the slightest ground for such an untruth. Everything between me and Sir Francis Geraldine was over before we had gone to the Continent. Why, I left England in consequence of the shock it gave me to have to abandon him. Does he know — does your brother know what I told you?'

'He did not know it when he wrote to me.'

'I suppose not. I should think he would send some message. As a rule he is soft-hearted, although to me he has become suddenly so inexpressibly cruel.'

'But you understand now the cause of his displeasure?'

'Not in the least,' said the angry wife. 'I know of no cause for his displeasure. Displeasure! I know of no cause to justify a step so terrible as this.'

'Though the statement may be untrue as you say —'

'It is untrue. It is altogether untrue.'

'But he has believed it!'

'Why has he believed it? Why; why?'

'Ah indeed; why?' said Lady Grant. 'I suppose that no lie becomes prevalent in the world for evil without some fault on the part of somebody. Even though it may not have been expressed in exact terms some false person has intentionally spread it abroad. And then a man in his wrath, when he hears the lie, will distort it, and twist it, and aggravate it, — to his own wrong and to that of others.'

'But my own husband! Him whom I so passionately loved!'

'And who so passionately loved you! It was because of that that the lie has so rankled! And, Cecilia, dear, let us be altogether open to each other.'

'I have concealed nothing from you,' said Mrs Western proudly.

'Nor wilfully from him. But you had kept from him a detail of your past life, — of your life not long since past, which, as you yourself felt, ought to have been made known to him.'

'It would have been made known to him.'

'Just so. But unfortunately he was first allowed to hear it from another quarter. How it was told from thence you and I do not know.'

'I saw the letter to him from Sir Francis Geraldine. There was no such statement in it as that you have now made. The tone of the letter was ungentlemanlike and abominable; but the facts as declared were true.'

'Do you believe then that he has invented this falsehood against you, to excuse himself?'

'No,' said the deserted wife; 'I do not think he invented it.'

'Nor I. How was it then that the idea has made its way into his brain?'

'He is suspicious,' said Mrs Western, speaking very slowly.

'Yes; he is suspicious. It is the fault of his character. But he is true and honest, and affectionate, and is by no means exacting or self-seeking. You have no right to expect that your husband should be perfect; — nor has he a right to expect it of you. He had no idea of this engagement till it was told by him who of all men was bound not to tell him.'

The conversation was carried on after this for a considerable time, but was left chiefly in the hands of Lady Grant. Two or three times Mrs Western put in a word, but it was always to ask what might be the effect upon him when he should have learned the tidings which she had sent him. Lady Grant seemed to think that he would of course come back and again take his wife to his bosom, as soon as he should be made to understand all the exact facts as to her intercourse with Sir Francis Geraldine and as to her quarrel with him. But poor Cecilia seemed to believe more in the coming of the little stranger. 'He can reject me,' she once said, with mingled bitterness and hope, 'but I cannot believe that such as he should reject his own child.'

But neither then nor on the following day, which was the last that Lady Grant allowed herself at Exeter, could she be induced to send to her husband a single word asking his pardon.

'No,' she said, holding her head aloft as she spoke; 'it is for me to pardon him. If he wants my pardon he shall have it. He need not ask for it, but if he comes he shall have it.'

Chapter XVII

MISS ALTIFIORLA RISES
IN THE WORLD

During this time a correspondence, more or less regular, was maintained between Miss Altifiorla and Sir Francis Geraldine. Sir Francis had gone to Scotland for the shooting, and rather liked the interest of Miss Altifiorla's letters. It must be understood that it had commenced with the lady rather than the gentleman. But that was a fact of which he was hardly aware. She had written him a short note in answer to some questions he had asked respecting Mrs Western when he had been in Exeter, and this she had done in such a manner as to make sure of the coming of a further letter. The further letter had come and thus the correspondence had been commenced. It was no doubt chiefly in regard to Mrs Western; or at first pretended to be so. Miss Altifiorla thought it right to speak always of her old friend with affectionate kindness; — but still with considerable severity. The affectionate kindness might go for what it was worth; but it was the severity or rather the sarcasm, which gratified Sir Francis. And then Miss Altifiorla gradually adopted a familiar strain into which Sir Francis fell readily enough. In fact Sir Francis found that a young woman who would joke with him, and appear to follow his lead in her joking, was more to his taste than an austere beauty such as had been his last love.

'Lady Grant is here at this moment,' Miss Altifiorla said in one of her letters. She had by this time fallen into that familiar style of writing which hardly declared whether it belonged to a man's letter or a woman's. 'I suppose you know who Lady Grant is. She is your fortunate rival's magnificent widowed sister, and has come here I presume to endeavour to set matters right. Whether she will succeed may be doubtful. She is the exact ditto of her brother, who of all human beings gives himself the finest airs. But Cecilia since her separation has given herself airs too, and now leads her lonely life with her nose high among the stars. Poor dear Cecilia; her misfortunes do not become her, and I think they have hardly been deserved. They are all the result of your bitter vengeance, and though I must say that she in sort deserves it, I think that you might have spared her. After all she has done you no harm. Consider where you would be with Cecilia Holt for your wife and guardian. Hard though you are, I do not think you would have been hard enough to treat her as he has done. Indeed there is an audacity about his conduct to which I know no parallel. Fancy a man marrying a wife and then instantly bidding her go home to her mother because he finds that she once liked another man better than himself! I wonder whether the law couldn't touch him! But you have escaped from all that, and I really can't understand why you should be so awfully cruel to the poor girl.' Then she signed herself 'Yours always, F.A.', as though she had not been a woman at all.

In all this there was much guile. She had already taken the length of his foot, and knew how to flatter him, and to cheat him at the same time. 'That poor young woman of mine seems to have got into difficulties,' he said to Dick Ross, who had gone down with him to Scotland.

'You have made the difficulties for her,' said Dick.

'Well; I paved the way perhaps. That was only justice. Did she think that she was going to hit me and that she wasn't to be hit in return?'

'A woman,' growled Dick.

'Women are human beings the same as men, and when they make themselves beasts have got to be punished. You can't horse-whip a woman; but if you look at it all round I don't see that she ought to get off so much better than a man. She is a human creature and ought to be made to feel as a man feels.'

But this did not suit Dick's morality or his sense of chivalry. According to his thinking a woman in such matters ought to be allowed to do as she pleased, and the punishment, if punishment there is to be, must come from the outside. 'I shouldn't like to have done it; that's all.'

'You've always treated women well; haven't you?'

'I don't say that. I don't know that I've ever treated anybody particularly well. But I never set my wits to work to take my revenge on a woman.'

'Look here, old fellow,' said Sir Francis. 'You had better contrive to make yourself less disagreeable or else you and I must part. If you think that I am going to be lectured by you, you're mistaken.'

'You ask me, and how can I help answering you? It was a shabby trick. And now you may bluster as much as you please.' Then the two sat together, smoking in silence for five minutes. It was after breakfast on a rainy day, such as always made Dick Ross miserable for the time. He had to think of creditors whom he could not pay and of his future life which did not lie easily open before him, and of all the years which he had misused. Circumstances had lately thrown him much into the power of this man whom he heartily disliked and despised, but at whose hands he had been willing to accept many of the luxuries of his life. But still he resolved not to be put down in the expression of his opinions although he might in truth be turned off at a moment's notice. 'You are corresponding with that old woman now?'

'What do you know about my correspondence?'

'I know just what you told me. That letter there is from the lady with the Italian name. She has more mischief even than you have, I believe.' At hearing this Sir Francis only laughed. 'If you don't take care she'll make you marry her, and then where will you be?'

'Where would you be, old fellow?'

'It don't much matter where I should be,' said poor Dick. 'There's a revolver upstairs and I sometimes think that I had better use it. I've nothing but myself to look after. I've no baronetcy and no estate, and can destroy none but myself. You can't hurt me very much. I'll tell you what it is, Geraldine. You want a wife so that you may cut out your cousin from the property. You're a good-looking fellow and you can talk, and, as chance would have it, you had, I imagine, got hold of a true lady. But she found you out.'

'What did she find out?'

'The sort of fellow that you are. She met you among the Dean's people, and had to find you out before she knew you. However she did before it was too late, and she gave you the sack.'

'That's your idea.'

'She did,' said Dick boldly. 'And there should have been an end of it. I don't say but what it might have been as well for you as for her. But it suited you to have your revenge, and you've had it.'

'I rather think I have,' said Sir Francis.

'But you've got a woman to help you in getting it who seems to have been as spiteful as you, without any excuse. I shouldn't think that she'd make a good wife. But if you don't take care she'll be yours.' Then Dick got up and walked out of the room with his pipe in his mouth, and

207

went into his bedroom, thinking that it might be as well for him to pack up and take his departure. The quarters they were in were, as he declared to himself, 'beastly' in wet weather; but his shirts hadn't come from the wash, and he had no vehicle to take him to the railway station without sending for a fly. And after all what he had said to Sir Francis was not much worse than what had often been said before. So he chucked off his slippers, and threw himself upon the bed thinking that he might as well endeavour to get through the morning by going to sleep.

Sir Francis when he found himself alone began to think over all the circumstances of his present position. Among those circumstances Dick Ross was one. When he had intended to marry Miss Holt he had determined to get rid of Dick. Indeed Dick had been got rid of partially, and had begun to talk of going to Canada or the Cannibal Islands, by way of beginning the work of his life. Then Sir Francis had been jilted, and Dick had again become indispensable to him. But Dick had ever had a nasty way of speaking his mind and blowing up his patron, which sometimes became very oppressive to the Baronet. And now at the present moment he was more angry with him for what he had said as to Miss Altifiorla than for his remarks as to his conduct to the other lady. All that was simply severe in Dick's words he took for a compliment. If Dick found fault with his practice he at any rate acknowledged his success. But his remarks as to the second lady had been very uncourteous. He had declared that she with the Italian name was a worse devil even than himself, and had warned him not to marry the fiend. Now he had nearly made up his mind that he would marry her. With all the ladies with whom he had hitherto been connected he had become aware that, in marrying them, he must more or less alter his manner of life. With Miss Altifiorla no such alteration would be necessary. He attributed a certain ease which she possessed to her Italian blood, and thought that he would be able to get on with her very comfortably. To marry was imperative with him, — because of his cousin. But he thought that were he to marry Miss Altifiorla he might continue to live his ordinary life almost without interruption. He had considered that in doing so he need not even dismiss Dick Ross. But now, in consequence partly of the great discourtesy of Dick's remarks and partly from his strong inclination for Miss Altifiorla, he began to think that after all Dick had better go. Just at this moment Dick's fortunes were, he knew, very low. One sum of money had been lost at cards, and another sum of money had not come. Dick's funds were almost absolutely worn out. But that was only a reason the more for parting with him. He did not care to have to deal with a man who had to wear out his old clothes in his house because he had not credit with his tailor to get a new coat and trousers. He thought that he would part with Dick; but he had not quite made up his mind when he sat down to write his letter to Miss Altifiorla.

'MY DEAR MISS ALTIFIORLA,' he said. 'I really don't see that you have any reason to blow me up as you do about "poor Cecilia". I do not think that poor Cecilia has had it at all hotter than she has deserved; and when you tell me that I have been awfully cruel to the poor girl, you seem to forget that the poor girl began the war by being awfully cruel to me. If you and I should ever come to know each other, you may be sure that I shall never treat any woman well because she has treated me badly. It's a kind of gallantry I cannot understand, and must make a man's conduct quite indifferent to the sex generally. If you're to treat all alike, whether they run straight or bolt, why shouldn't they all bolt? It would come to the same thing in the end. There is Dick Ross been making himself uncommonly disagreeable on the same subject. I don't mind your lecturing me a little, — chiefly because you don't think it; but I'll be hanged if I take it from him. He has not done so very well himself that he is entitled to blow up any one.

'Mind you write and tell me what happens over at St David's.' Mrs Holt lived in Exeter at St David's. 'I shall be glad to know whether that respectable person, Mr Western, comes back again. I don't think she'll have a good time if he does, and if he don't I sha'n't break my heart.' Then he put his pen down and sat for a while thinking what should be his last paragraph.

Should he put an end to all his doubts and straightway make his offer, or should he dally a little longer and still keep the power in his own hands? At last he said to himself that even if he wrote it his letter would not go till to-morrow morning, and he would have the night to think about it. This consideration got the better of his prudence and he did write it, simply beginning a new sentence on the page. 'Don't you think that you and I know each other well enough to make a match of it? There is a question for you to answer on your own behalf, instead of blowing me up for any cruelty to Cecilia Holt.'

Then he signed his name, 'Yours ever, F.G.'

Miss Altifiorla when she received the letter was surprised, but not startled. She had expected that it would come, but not so quickly; and it may be said of her that she had quite made up her mind as to the final answer to be given if it should come. But still she had to think much about it before she wrote her reply. It might be very well for him to be sudden, but any over-suddenness on her part would put him on his guard. If he should be made to feel alarmed at what he had done, if he should be once frightened at his own impetuousness and hers, he would soon find his way back again out of the difficulty. But still she must flatter him, still she must make him think that she loved him. It would not at all do for her to write as though the thing were impossible. Then in a pleasant reverie she gave herself up for a while to meditating over the sudden change which had come upon her views of life. She remembered how strong she had been in recommending Cecilia not to marry this man, and how she had congratulated her when she found that she had escaped. And she remembered the severe things she had said about Mr Western. But in her thoughts there was nothing of remorse or even of regret. 'Well, well; that it should have come to this! That he should have escaped from Cecilia and have chosen me! Upon the whole it will be much better for him. I shall tread on his corns less than she would, and be less trodden upon, too, than she. It may be that I must tread on his corns a little, but I will not begin till after my marriage.' Such was the nature of her thoughts. Perhaps an idea did creep in as to some awkwardness when she should meet Cecilia. But they could never see much of each other, and it might be that there would be no such meeting. 'What does it matter?' she said, as she turned to her writing-table.

But this was not till three days had passed after the receipt of the proposal. Three days, she thought, was a fitting time to show that though hurried by an affair of so much moment, she was not too much hurried. And then she wrote as follows; —

'MY DEAR SIR FRANCIS,
'Your letter has almost taken away my breath. Why, you know nothing or little

about me! And since we have been acquainted with each other our conversation has chiefly been about another lady to whom you were engaged to be married. Now you ask me to be your wife; at least, if I understand your letter, that is its purport. If I am wrong, of course you will tell me so.

'But of course I know that I am not wrong; and of course I am flattered, and of course pleased. What I have seen of you I have altogether liked, and I do not know why we should not be happy together. But, marriage! marriage is a most important step, — as, no doubt, you are well aware. Though I am quite earnest in what I am saying, still I cannot but smile, and can fancy that you are smiling, as though after all it were but a joke. However, give me but one week to think of it all and then I will answer you in sober earnest.

'Yours ever (as you sign yourself),
'F.A.'

Chapter XVIII

A MAN'S PRIDE

About a week after Lady Grant had gone Mrs Western received a letter from her husband. She had expected that he would write, and had daily looked for the letter. But when it did come she did not know whether to take it as a joy or a source of additional discomfort. There was in it hardly a word of declared affection. Nothing was said as to his future life or hers; but he did write, as she thought, in a familiar and loving strain as to the event which had yet to be expected for many months. 'My sister has told me your news,' he said, 'and I cannot but let you know how anxious I shall be both for your safety and for that of the stranger. If there be anything that I can do for your comfort, if you will ask me, you may be sure that it will be done. I am still at Dresden, and have no idea of immediately returning to England.' There was no commencement to this, nor any ending. He did not even sign his name, nor call her his wife, or his dear Cecilia. Upon the whole she felt that it rather confirmed her sentence of banishment than gave her reason for hope. He had felt when he wrote it that he could not remain altogether silent, but had yet determined to awaken no hopes by an assurance of his returning love. 'In fact, the letter,' she said to her mother, 'must be taken as meaning nothing. He did not choose to subject himself to the charge of having been indifferent to the coming of such an event. But beyond this he had had nothing to say to me.' Poor Mrs Holt remained altogether silent when her daughter discussed the subject. She knew that she could not speak without loud abuse, and she knew also that her daughter would not allow her to abuse him.

Cecilia, without asking the advice of any one, resolved that she would not answer the letter. She could not write without using affectionate language, and such words should never come from her till she had first been addressed with full affection by him. 'Never,' she had said to herself a score of times; 'never!' The meaning of this had been that having been so cruelly ill-used she would do and say nothing that might be taken as evidence that she had thought herself in the wrong. She would bear it all, rather than give him to understand that she did not appreciate his cruelty. She had told him of her love, and he had not vouchsafed to say a word to her in reply. It was of the injustice done to her that she complained in the words which she was constantly framing for herself; but it was the apparent want of affection which was deepest in her heart. Though he had been twice as cruel, twice as hard, she would have been less unhappy had she succeeded in drawing from him one word of affection. 'What can he do for my comfort?' she said to herself again and again. 'He means that if

I want money I shall have it, so that he may avoid the disgrace of leaving his wife and his child unprovided for. I will not have his money, unless he also come himself.' She would not even write to Lady Grant, or let her know that she had received a letter from her husband. 'Oh, yes; I have heard from him. There is his letter,' and she flung the document across the table to her mother. Having done so she at once left the room, so that there should be no discussion on the matter. 'That there should be not a word of love in it; not a single word,' she went on saying to herself. 'How hard must be a man's heart, and how changeable! He certainly did love me, and now it has all gone, simply through an unworthy suspicion on his own part.'

But here she showed how little able she had been as yet to read the riddle of a man's heart, — how ignorant she had been of the difficulty under which a man may labour to express his own feeling! That which we call reticence is more frequently an inability than an unwillingness to express itself. The man is silent, not because he would not have the words spoken, but because he does not know the fitting words with which to speak. His dignity and his so-called manliness are always near to him, and are guarded, so that he should not melt into open ruth. So it was with Mr Western. Living there all alone at Dresden, seeing no society, passing much of his time in a vain attempt to satisfy himself with music and with pictures, he spent all his hours in thinking how necessary his wife had made herself to his comfort during the few months that they were married. He had already taught himself to endeavour to make excuses for her, — though in doing so he always fell back at last on the enormity of her offence. Though he loved her, though he might probably pardon her in his weakness, it was impossible that the sin should be washed out. His anger still burned very hotly, because he could not quite understand the manner in which the sin had been committed. There was a secret, and he did not know the nature of the secret. There had been an understanding, of which he did not even yet know the nature, between his wife and that base baronet. And then the terrible truth of his memory added to his wounds. He thought of all the words that had been spoken, and which he felt ought to have given her an opportunity of telling the truth, — and would have done so had she not purposely kept the secret. He had playfully asked her how it had been that she had loved no other man, and then she had remained silent in a manner which he now declared to himself to be equal to a falsehood. And when he had been perfectly free with his own story, she had still kept back hers. She had had her story, and had resolved that he should not know it, even though he had been so open with his. He no doubt had been open at a time when he had no right to expect her to be equally so; but when the time did come, then she had been a traitor to him. When accepting his caresses and returning them with all a young wife's ardour, even at that moment she had been a traitor to him. Though in his arms she had thought, — she must have continued to think, — of some unholy compact which existed between her and Sir Francis Geraldine. And even now she had not told him the nature of that compact. Even now she might be corresponding with Sir Francis or seeing him for aught that he knew to the contrary. How was it possible that he should pardon a wife who had sinned against him as she had sinned?

And yet he was so far aware of his own weakness as to admit to himself that he would have taken her back to him if she had answered his last letter in a contrite spirit and with affectionate words. He would have endeavoured to forget if not to forgive, and would have allowed himself to fall into the loving intimacy of domestic life, — but that she was cold and indifferent as well as treacherous. So he told himself, keeping his wrath hot, though at the same time his love nearly mastered him. But in truth he knew nothing of things as they really were. He had made the mistake of drawing a false conclusion from some words written by Sir Francis, and then of looking upon those words as containing the whole truth. Sir Francis had no doubt intended him to think that he and Cecilia Holt had come to some rupture in their engagement from other than the real cause. He had intended Mr Western to believe that they had both agreed, and that they had merely resolved between them that they had better not be husband and wife. He had intended to convey the idea that he had been more active in so arranging it than Cecilia herself. Cecilia, though she had read the letter, had done so in such a frame of mind as hardly to catch the truth. But he, Mr Western, had caught it altogether and had believed it. Though he knew that the man was a dishonest liar yet he had believed the letter. He was tortured at the thought that his wife should have made herself a party to such a compact, and that the compact should still have remained in existence without his knowledge. Although there were hours during which he was most anxious to return to her, — in which he told himself that it was more difficult to stay away from her than even to endure her faithlessness; though from day to day he became convinced that he could never return to the haunts of men or even to the easy endurance of life without her, yet his pride would ever come back to him and assure him that as a reasonable man he was unable to put up with such treachery. He had unfortunately been taught to think, by the correspondence which had come from the matter of his cousin's racing bet, that Sir Francis Geraldine was the very basest of mankind. It was unfortunate, for he had no doubt been induced to think worse of his wife because she had submitted herself and continued to submit herself to a man who was in his eyes so contemptible. He could not endure the idea that a woman for whom such a partnership had had charms should be the chosen companion of all his hours. He had already lived with her for weeks which should have been enough to teach him her character. During those weeks he had been satisfied to the very full. He had assured himself frequently that he had at last met a woman that suited him and made her his own. Had he known nothing of Sir Francis Geraldine he would have been thoroughly contented. Then had come the blow, and all his joys were 'sicklied over' with the unhealthy tone which his image of her former lover gave him. She became at once to him a different creature. Though he told himself that she was still the same Cecilia as had been his delight, yet he told himself also that she was not the same as he had fancied her when he at first knew her.

There is in a man a pride of which a woman knows nothing. Or rather a woman is often subject to pride the very opposite. The man delights to think that he has been the first to reach the woman's heart; the woman is rejoiced to feel that she owns permanently that which has been often reached before. The man may know that in his own case it is not so with him. But as there has been no concealment, or perhaps only a little to conceal, he takes it as it comes and makes the best of it. His Mary may have liked some other one, but it has not gone farther. Or if she has been engaged as a bride there has been no secret about it. Or it has been a thing long ago, so that there has been time for new ideas to form themselves. The husband when he does come knows at any rate that he has no ground of complaint, and is not kept specially in the dark when he takes his wife. But Mr Western had been kept specially in the dark, and was of all men the least able to endure such treatment. To have been kept in the dark as to the man with whom the girl was engaged, as he thought, at the very moment in which she had accepted him! To have been made use of as a step, on which a disadvantageous marriage might be avoided without detriment to her own interest! It was this feeling which made him utterly prostrate, — which told him that death itself would be the one desirable way out of his difficulties if death were within his reach.

When he received the letter from his sister telling him that he might probably become the father of a child, he was at the first prepared to say that thus would they two be reconciled. He could hardly live apart, not only from the mother of his child, but from the child itself. He went away into solitude and wept hot tears as he thought of it all. But ever as he thought of it the cause of his anger came back to him and made him declare to himself that in the indulgence of no feeling of personal tenderness ought he to disgrace himself. At any rate it could not be till she should have told him the whole truth, — till she should have so told her story as to enable him to ascertain whether that story were in all respects true. At present, as he said to himself, he was altogether in the dark. But in fact had he now learned the very story as it had existed, and had Cecilia told it as far as she was able to tell it at all, she would even in his estimation have been completely whitewashed. In her perfect absolution from the terrible sin of which he now accused her he would have forgiven and forgotten altogether the small, the trifling fault, which she had in truth committed.

There was something of nobility in all these feelings; — but then that something was alloyed by much that was ignoble. He had resolved that were she to come back to him she must come acknowledging the depth of her sin. He would endeavour to forgive though he could not forget; but he never thought in these hours that it would be well for him to be gracious in his manner of forgiveness. To go to her and fetch her home to him, and say to her that all that was past should be as a dream, a sad and ugly dream, but one to which no reality was attached, never occurred to him. He must still be the master, and, in order that his masterdom might be assured, full and abject confession must be made. Yet he had such an idea of his wife, that he felt that no such confession would be forthcoming, and therefore to him it appeared ever more and more impossible that they two should again come together.

With Cecilia the matter was regarded with very different eyes. To her, too, it was apparent that she had been treated with extremest cruelty.

She, too, was very hot in her anger. In discussing the matter with herself, she allowed herself thoughts in which indignation against her husband was maintained at a boiling heat. But nevertheless she had quite resolved to forgive him altogether if he would once come to her. And to insure her forgiveness no word even of apology should be necessary. She knew that she would have to deal with a man to whom the speaking of such words would be painful, and none should be expected, none asked for. If he would but show her that he still loved her, that should suffice. The world around them would of course know that she had been sent away from him, and then taken back. There was in this much that was painful, — a feeling full of dismay as she reflected that all her friends, that her acquaintance, that the very servants should know that she had been so disgraced. But of all that she would take no notice, — no notice as far as the outside world was concerned. Let them think, let them talk as they would, she would then have her one great treasure with which to console herself, and that would suffice for her happiness. In her hottest anger she told herself from time to time that her anger would all depart from her, — that it would be made to vanish from her as by a magician's wand, — if she could only once more be allowed to feel his arm round her waist.

In all this she had no friend with whom to discuss either her anger or her hopes. Her mother she knew shared her anger to the full, but entertained hopes altogether different. Her desires were so different that they hardly amounted to hopes. Yes, he might be allowed to return, but with words of absolute contrition, with words which should always be remembered against him. Such would have been Mrs Holt's expression as to the state of things had she ventured to express herself. But she understood enough of her daughter's feelings to repress them.

The only person who sympathised with Cecilia and her present condition was the girl who had once before evoked from her so strong a feeling of tenderness. She did know that the man had to be forgiven, terrible as had been his sin, and that nothing more was to be said about it. 'Oh, ma'am,' she said, 'he'll come back now. I'm sure he'll come back now, and never more have any of them silly vagaries.'

'Who can say what vagaries a man may choose to indulge?'

'That's true too, ma'am. That any man should have had such a vagary as this! But he's dying to come back. I'm sure of it. And when he does come and finds that he's let to come quiet, and that he's asked to say nothing as he don't like, and that you are all smiles to him and kindness, — and then with the baby coming and all, — my belief is that he'll be happier then than he was even the first day when he had you.' This, though spoken in rough language, so exactly expressed Cecilia's wishes, that she did feel that her maid at least entirely sympathised with her.

Chapter XIX

DICK TAKES
HIS FINAL LEAVE

When Sir Francis received the reply which Miss Altifiorla sent to his letter, he was not altogether satisfied with it. He had expected that the lady would at once have flown into his arms. But the lady seemed to hesitate, and asked for a week to think about it. This showed so much ingratitude on her part, — was so poor an acknowledgment of the position which he had offered her, that he was inclined to be indignant. 'If she don't care about it she shan't have it.' It was thus that he expressed himself aloud in the hearing of Dick Ross; but without however explaining who the 'she' was, or what the 'it' was, or indeed in any way asking Dick's opinion on the matter. Not the less had Miss Altifiorla been wise in the nature of the reply which she had given. Had she expressed her warm affection, and at once accepted all that had been proffered, the gentleman would probably have learnt at once to despise that which had been obtained so easily. As it was he was simply cross, and thought that he had determined to withdraw the proposal. But still the other letter was to come, and Miss Altifiorla's chance was still open to her.

The immediate consequence of these doubts in the mind of Sir Francis was a postponement of the verdict of banishment which he had resolved to pronounce against Dick as soon as his marriage with Miss Altifiorla should have been settled. He did not wish to leave himself altogether alone in the world, and if this Dick were dismissed it would be necessary that he should provide himself with another, — unless he were minded to provide himself with a wife instead. He became therefore gradually more gracious after the little speech which has been above given. Dick had understood perfectly who the 'she' had been, and what was the 'it' intended. As no question had been asked he had made no reply, but he was quite quick enough to perceive the working of the Baronet's mind. He despised the Baronet almost as thoroughly as did Mr Western. But for certain purposes, — as to which he despised himself also, — the friendship of the Baronet suited him just at present.

One morning, for private reasons of his own, Dick went into Perth, which was twenty miles distant from the Baronet's shooting lodge, and returned the same day bringing the postbag with him from a point in the road at which it was daily left by the postman. Sir Francis with unusual haste read his letters, and among them was one from Miss Altifiorla. But Dick had a budget of news which he was anxious to reveal, and which he did tell before Sir Francis had said anything as to his own letter. There was another friend, one Captain Fawkes, at the Lodge with them, and Dick had at first been restrained by this man's presence. As soon as he found himself alone with

Sir Francis he began. 'Lady Grant has gone off to Dresden,' he said.

'Where did you hear that?' asked the Baronet.

'They told me so at the club. Everybody in Perth knows that she has gone; — and why.'

'What business is it of theirs? Since you know so much about it, why has she gone?'

'To persuade her brother to come home and take his wife once more. It was a great shame that they should ever have been separated. In fact she has gone to undo what you did. If she can only succeed in making the man know the whole truth about it, free from all lies, she'll do what she's gone to do.'

'What the devil do you mean by lies?' said Sir Francis, rising in wrath from his chair.

'Well; lies mean lies. As I haven't applied the word to any one I suppose I may be allowed to use it and to stand by it. I suppose you know what lies mean, and I suppose you are aware that Western has been made to believe lies about his wife.'

'Who told them?'

'I say nothing about that,' said Dick. 'Lies are a sort of thing which are very commonly told, and are ordinarily ascribed to the world at large. The world never quarrels with the accusation. The world has told most infernal lies to this man about his wife. I don't suppose the world means to call me out for saying as much as that.' Then the two remained silent for some moments and Dick proceeded with his eloquence. 'Of course there have been lies, — wretched lies. Had a man, or a woman — it's all one, — gone to that poor creature with a pistol in his hand and blown her brains out he wouldn't have done a more dastardly action.'

'What the mischief do you mean by that?' said the other.

'I'm not talking about you, — specially. I say lies have been told; but I do not say who has told them. I rather suspect a woman to be at the bottom of it.' Sir Francis, who had in his pocket a most tender and loving reply from Miss Altifiorla, knew very well who was the lady to whom Dick referred. 'That man has been made to believe certain things about his wife which are all lies, — lies from beginning to end.'

'He has been made to believe that she was engaged to me first. Is that a lie?'

'That depends on the way in which it was told. He didn't send her home merely for that. I am not saying what the lies were, but there were wicked lies. You sometimes tell me that I ain't any better than another, — or, generally, a great deal worse. But I'd rather have blown my brains out than have told such lies about a woman as have been told here by somebody. You ask me what they were saying at the club in Perth. Now you know it pretty well all.'

It must be supposed that what had passed at the club had induced Dick to determine that it would no longer become him to remain with Sir Francis as his humble friend. Very evil things had in truth been said of Sir Francis, and they were more than Dick could endure. The natural indignation of the man was aroused, so that by degrees it had come to pass that he hated the Baronet. He had before said very sharp words to him, but had now gone home resolved in his righteous mind to bring things to a conclusion. It matters little in the telling of our story to know what lies Dick did in truth impute to his friend; but they were of a nature to fill his mind with righteous wrath and to produce from him the eloquence above described.

Sir Francis, whose vanity had been charmed by the letter which he kept in his pocket, had already made up his mind to part with Dick. But Dick's words as now spoken left him no alternative. It was a question with him whether he could not so part with him as to inflict some further punishment. 'Why, Dick,' he said smiling, 'you have broken out quite in a new place.'

'I know nothing about that.'

'You must have been with the Bishop and taken a lesson in preaching. I never heard you come out so strong before.'

'I wish you'd heard what some of those men at Perth said about you.'

'And how you answered them, — as my friend.'

'As far as I remember I didn't say much myself. What I did say certainly was not in your favour. But I was hardest on that sweet young lady with the Italian name. You won't mind that because you and she are two, now.'

'Can you tell me, Ross, how long you have been eating my bread?'

'I suppose I could.'

'Or how much you have drunk of my wine?'

'I haven't made a calculation of that nature. It isn't usual.'

'For shooting here, how much have you ever contributed?'

'When I shoot I contribute nothing. All the world understands that.'

'How much money do you owe me?'

'I owe you nothing that I've ever promised to pay.'

'And now you think it a sign of a fine gentleman to go and talk openly at a club about matters which you have heard from me in confidence! I don't. I think it a very —'

'A very what, Sir Francis? I have not done as you allege. But you were going to observe a very — ; what was it?' It must be here explained that Dick Ross was not a man who feared many things; but that Sir Francis feared much. Dick had little to lose by a row, whereas the Baronet would be injured. The Baronet therefore declined to fill in the epithet which he had omitted. He knew from former experience what Dick would and what he would not bear.

'I don't choose to descend to Billingsgate,' said Sir Francis. 'I have my own ideas as to your conduct.'

'Very gentlemanlike, isn't it?' said Dick, with a

smile, meaning thereby to impute it to Sir Francis as cowardice that he was unwilling to say the reverse.

'But under all the circumstances, it will be quite as well that you should leave the Lodge. You must feel that yourself.'

'Oh; quite so. I am delighted to think that I shall be able to leave without having had any unpleasant words. Perhaps to-morrow will do?'

'Just as you please.'

'Then I shall be able to add a few glasses to all those buckets of claret which you threw in my teeth just now. I wonder whether any gentleman was ever before asked by another gentleman how much wine he had drunk in his house, or how many dinners he had eaten. When you asked me did you expect me to pay for my dinners and wine?' Sir Francis refused to make any reply to this question. 'And when you delicately hinted at my poverty, had you found my finances to be lower than you'd always known them? It is disagreeable to be a penniless younger brother. I have found it so all my life. And I admit that I ought to have earned my bread. It would have been much better for me had I done so. People may declare that I am good for nothing, and may hold me up as an example to be shunned. But I flatter myself that nobody has called me a blackguard. I have told no lies to injure men behind their backs; — much less have I done so to injure a woman. I have sacrificed no girl to my revenge, simply because she has thrown me over. In the

231

little transactions I have had I have always run straight. Now I think that upon the whole, I had better go before dinner and not add anything to the buckets of claret.'

'Just as you please,' said Sir Francis. Then Dick Ross left the room and went away to make such arrangements for his departure as were possible to him, and the readers of this story shall see him and hear him no more.

Sir Francis when he was left alone took out Miss Altifiorla's letter and read it again. He was a man who could assume grand manners in his personal intercourse with women, but was peculiarly apt to receive impressions from them. He loved to be flattered, and was prone to believe anything good of himself that was said to him by one of them. He therefore took the following letter for more than it was worth.

'MY DEAR SIR FRANCIS,
'I know that you will have been quite quick enough to have understood when you received my former little scrawl what my answer would be. When a woman attempts to deceive a man in such a matter she knows beforehand that the attempt will be vain; and I certainly did not think that I could succeed with you. But yet a feeling of shamefacedness, — what some ladies consider as modesty, though it might more properly be called *mauvaise honte,* — forced me into temporary silence. What could I wish better than to be

loved by such a one as you? In the first place there is the rank which goes for much with me. Then there is the money, which I admit counts for something. I would never have allowed myself to marry even if I had chanced to love a poor man. Then there are the manners, and the peculiar station before the world which is quite separate from the rank. To me these alone are irresistible. Shall I say too that personal appearance does count for much. I can fancy myself marrying an ugly man, but I can fancy also that I could not do it without something of disgust.' Miss Altifiorla when she wrote this had understood well that vanity and love of flattery were conspicuous traits in the character of her admirer. 'Having owned so much what is there more to say than that I am the happiest woman between the seas?'

The reader must be here told that this letter had been copied out a second time because in the first copy she had allowed the word girl to pass in the above sentence. Something told her that she had better write woman instead, and she had written it.

'What more is there for me to add to the above except to tell you that I love you with all my heart. Months ago, — it seems to be years now, — when Cecilia Holt had caught your fancy, I did regard her as the most fortunate girl. But I did not regard you as the happiest of men, because I felt sure that there was a something between you which would not suit. There is an asperity, rather than strictness, about her which I knew your spirit would not brook. She would have borne the battlings which would have arisen with an equal temper. She can indeed bear all things with equanimity, — as she does her present position. But you, though you would have battled and have conquered, would still have suffered. I do not think that the wife you now desire is one with whom you will have to wage war. Shall I say that if you marry her whom you have now asked to join her lot with yours, there will be no such fighting. I think that I shall know how to hold my own against the world as your wife. But with you I shall only attempt to hold my own by making myself one with you in all your desires and aspirations.

'I am yours with all my heart, and with all my body and soul.

'FRANCISCA.

'I say nothing now about the immediate future, but I hope it will please your Highness to visit your most worthy clerical relations in this cathedral city before long. I shall say nothing to any of your clerical relations as to my prospects in life until I shall have received your sanction for doing so. But the sooner I do receive it the better for my peace of mind.'

Sir Francis was upon the whole delighted with the letter, and the more delighted as he now read it for the third time. 'There is such an air of truth in every word of it.' It was thus that he spoke to himself about the letter as he sucked in the flattery. It was thus that Miss Altifiorla had intended that he should receive it. She knew herself too well to suspect that her flattery should fail. Not a word of it failed. In nothing was he more gratified than in her allusions to his matrimonial efforts with Miss Holt. She had assured him that he would have finally conquered that strong-minded young woman. But she had at the same time told him of the extreme tenderness of his heart. He absolutely believed her when she whispered to him her secret, — that she had envied Cecilia her lot when Cecilia was supposed to be the happy bride. He quite understood those allusions to his own pleasures and her assurance that she would never interfere with him. There was just a doubt whether a thing so easily got could be worth the keeping. But then he remembered his cousin and determined to be a man of his word.

Chapter XX

THE SECRET ESCAPES

'All right. See you soon. Ever yours, F.G.' Such was the entire response which Miss Altifiorla received from her now declared lover. Sir Francis had told himself that he hated the bother of writing love-letters. But in truth there was with him also an idea that it might be as well that he should not commit himself to declarations that were in their nature very strong. It was not that he absolutely thought of any possible future event in which his letters might be used against him, but there was present to him a feeling that the least said might be the soonest mended.

Miss Altifiorla when she received the above scrawl was quite satisfied with it. She, too, was cautious in her nature, but not quite so clever as her lover. She did, indeed, feel that she had now caught her fish. She would not let him escape by any such folly as that which Cecilia Holt had committed. The Baronet should be allowed his full swing till she was entitled to call herself Lady Geraldine. Then, perhaps, there might be a tussle between them as to which should have his own way, — or hers. The great thing at present was to obtain the position, and she did feel that she had played her cards uncommonly well as far as the game had gone at present.

But there came upon her an irresistible temptation to make her triumph known among her friends at Exeter. All her girl friends had got themselves married. There was Mrs Green, and Mrs Thorne, and Mrs Western. Poor Cecilia had not gained much, but still she was Mrs Western. Miss Altifiorla did in truth regard herself as Miss Altifiorla with but small satisfaction. She had her theories about women's rights, and the decided advantages of remaining single, and the sufficiency of a lady to stand alone in the world. There was probably some vague glimmering of truth in her ideas; some half-formed belief in her own doctrine. But still it had ever been an uncomfortable creed, and one which she was ready to desert at the slightest provocation. Her friends had all deserted it, and had left her as we say high and dry on the barren bank, while they had been carried away by the fertilising stream. She, too, would now swim down the river of matrimony with a beautiful name, and a handle to it, as the owner of a fine family property. Women's rights was an excellent doctrine to preach, but for practice could not stand the strain of such temptation. And, though in boasting of her good fortune, she must no doubt confess that she had been wrong, still there would be much more of glory than of shame in the confession.

It was chance probably that made her tell her secret in the first instance to Mrs Thorne. Mrs Thorne had been Maude Hippesley and was niece to Sir Francis Geraldine. Miss Altifiorla had pledged herself to Sir Francis not to make known her engagement at the Deanery. But such pledges go for very little. Mrs Thorne was not now an inhabitant of Exeter, and was, so to say, the most bosom-friend left to her, — after her disruption from Mrs Western. Was it probable that such a secret should be kept from a bosom-friend? Mrs Thorne, who had a large circle of friends in the county, would hardly have admitted the claim, but she would be more likely to do so after receiving the intimation. Of course it would be conveyed under the seal of a sacred promise, — which no doubt would be broken as soon as she reached the Deanery. On this occasion she called on Miss Altifiorla to ask questions in reference to 'poor Cecilia'. With herself, and the Dean and Mrs Dean there was real sorrow at Cecilia's troubles. And there was also no mode of acquiring true information. 'Do tell me something about poor Cecilia,' said Mrs Thorne.

'Poor Cecilia, indeed! She is there all alone and sees almost no one. Of course you've heard that Lady Grant was here.'

'We thought it so nice of Lady Grant to come all the way from Scotland to see her sister-in-law.'

'Lady Grant of course is anxious to get her brother to take back his wife. They haven't a great deal of money among them, and when Mrs Holt dies Cecilia's fortune would be a nice addition.'

'I don't think Lady Grant can have thought of that,' said Mrs Thorne.

'Lady Grant would be quite prudent in thinking of it and like the rest of the world. Her husband was only a regimental officer in India who got knighted for doing something that came in his way. There isn't any family property among them, and of course she is anxious.'

This solicitude as to 'family property' on the part of Miss Altifiorla did strike Mrs Thorne as droll. But she went on with her inquiries. 'And what is Cecilia doing?'

'Not very much,' said Miss Altifiorla. 'What is there for her to do? Poor girl. She has played her cards so uncommonly badly, when she took up with Mr Western after having been dropped by Sir Francis.'

'After dropping Sir Francis!'

Miss Altifiorla smiled. Was it likely that Cecilia Holt should have dropped Sir Francis? 'It doesn't much matter now. If it does her wounded pride good to say so of course she can say it.'

'We always believed that it was so at the Deanery.'

'At any rate she made a mess of it. And now she has to bear the fortune which her fates have sent her. I own that I am a little angry with Cecilia, not for having dropped Sir Francis, as you called it, but for managing her matters so badly with Mr Western. She seems to me to have no idea of the sort of duties which fall to the lot of a wife.'

'I should have thought you'd have liked her the better for that,' said Mrs Thorne, with a smile.

'Why so? I think you must have misunderstood my theory of life. When a woman elects to marry, and does so from sheer love and regard for the man, she should certainly make her duty to him the first motive of all her actions.'

'What a grand lesson! It is a pity that my husband should not be here to hear it.'

'I have no doubt he finds that you do so.'

'Or Sir Francis Geraldine. I suppose my uncle is still in search of a wife, and if he knew where to find such excellent principles he would be able to make his choice. What a joke it would be should he again try his luck at Exeter!'

'He has again tried his luck at Exeter,' said Miss Altifiorla in a tone in which some slight shade of ridicule was mixed with the grandiloquence which she wished to assume.

'What on earth do you mean?' said Mrs Thorne.

'Simply what I seem to mean. I had not intended to have told you at present, though I would sooner tell you than any person living. You must promise me, however, that it shall go no further. Sir Francis Geraldine has done me the honour to ask me to be his wife.' Thus she communicated her good news; and did so in a tone of voice that was very low, and intended to be humble.

'My uncle going to marry you? Good gracious!'

'Is it more wonderful than that he should have thought of marrying Cecilia Holt?'

'Well, yes. Not that I know why it should be, except that Cecilia came first, and that you and she were so intimate.'

'Was he doomed to remain alone in the world because of that?' asked Miss Altifiorla.

'Well, no; I don't exactly mean that. But it is droll.'

'I hope that the Dean and Mrs Hippesley will be satisfied with his choice. I do particularly hope that all his friends will feel that he is doing well. But,' she added, perceiving that her tidings had not been received with any strong expression of family satisfaction — 'but I trust that, as Lady Geraldine, I may at any rate be the means of keeping the family together.'

There was to Mrs Thorne almost a joke in this, as she knew that her father did not at all approve of Sir Francis, and was with difficulty induced to have him at the Deanery. And she knew also that the Dean did in his heart greatly dislike Miss Altifiorla, though for the sake of what was generally called 'peace within the cathedral precincts', he had hitherto put up also with her. What might happen in the Dean's mind, or what determination the Dean might take when the two should be married, she could not say. But she felt that it might probably be beyond the power of the future Lady Geraldine 'to keep the family together'. 'Well, I am surprised,' said Mrs Thorne. 'And I am to tell nobody.'

'I don't see any good in publishing the thing in High Street just at present.' Then Mrs Thorne understood that she need not treat the communication as a strict secret. 'In fact, I don't see why it should be kept specially in the dark. Francis has not enjoined anything like secrecy.' This was the first time that she had allowed herself the use of the Baronet's name without the prefix. 'When it is to be I have not as yet even begun to think. Of course he is in a hurry. Men, I believe, generally are. But in this case there may be some reasons for delay. Arrangements as to the family property must be made, and Castle Gerald must be prepared for our reception. I don't suppose we can be married just off hand, like some happier folks.' Mrs Thorne did not know whether to take this to herself, as she had been married herself, at last, rather in a scramble, or whether it was intended to apply to poor Cecilia, whose husband, though he was in comfortable circumstances, cannot be said to have possessed family property. 'And now, dear,' continued Miss Altifiorla, 'what am I to do for bridesmaids? You three have all been married before me. There are his two unmarried sisters of course.' Mrs Thorne was aware that her uncle had absolutely quarrelled with his mother and sisters, and had not spoken to them for years. 'I suppose that it will come off in the cathedral, and that your father will perform the ceremony. I don't know, indeed, whether Francis might not wish to have the Bishop.' Mrs

Thorne was aware that the Bishop, who was a strict man, would not touch Sir Francis Geraldine with a pair of tongs. 'But all these things will shake themselves down comfortably no doubt. In the meantime I am in a twitter of ecstatic happiness. You who have gone through it all will quite understand what I mean. It seems that as a lover he is the most exigeant of gentlemen. He requires constant writing to, and woe betide me if I do not obey his behests. However, I do not complain, and must confess that I am at the present moment the most happy of young women.'

Mrs Thorne of course expressed her congratulations and took her departure without having committed herself to a word as to the other inhabitants of the Deanery. But when she got to her father's house, where she was for the present staying, she in truth startled them all by the news. The Dean had just come into the drawing-room to have his afternoon tea and a little gossip with his wife and his own sister, Mrs Forrester, from London. 'Who do you think is going to be married, and to whom?' said Mrs Thorne. 'I'll give you all three guesses a piece, and bet you a pair of gloves all round that you don't make it out.'

'Not Miss Altifiorla?' said her mother.

'That's only one. A marriage requires two personages. I still hold good by my bet.'

'Miss Altifiorla going to be married!' said the Dean. 'Who is the unfortunate victim?'

'Papa, do not be ill-natured. Why should not Miss Altifiorla be married as well as another?'

'In the first place, my dear,' said Mrs Forrester, 'because I understand that the lady has always expressed herself as being in favour of a single life.'

'I go beyond that,' said the Dean, 'and maintain that any single life would be preferable to a marriage with Miss Altifiorla.'

'Considering that she is my friend, papa, I think that you are very unkind.'

'But who is to be the gentleman?' asked her mother.

'Ah, there's the question! Why don't you guess?' Then Mrs Dean did name three or four of the most unpromising unmarried elderly gentlemen in Exeter, and the Dean, in that spirit of satire against his own order which is common among clergymen, suggested an old widowed Minor Canon, who was in the habit of chanting the Litany.

'You are none of you near the mark. You ought to come nearer home.'

'Nearer home?' said Mrs Dean with a look of discomfort in her face.

'Yes, mamma. A great deal nearer home.'

'It can't be your Uncle Septimus,' said the Dean. Now Uncle Septimus was the unmarried brother of old Mr Thorne, and was regarded by all the Thorne family as a perfect model of an unselfish, fine old loveable gentleman.

'Good gracious, no!' said Mrs Thorne. 'What

a horrible idea! Fancy Uncle Septimus doomed to pass his life in company with Miss Altifiorla! The happy man in question is — Sir Francis Geraldine.'

'No!' said Mrs Hippesley, jumping from her seat.

'It is impossible,' said the Dean, who though he greatly disliked his brother-in-law still thought something of the family into which he had married and thoroughly despised Miss Altifiorla. 'I do not think that Sir Francis could be so silly as that.'

'It cannot be,' said Mrs Hippesley.

'What has the young lady done to make it impossible?' asked Mrs Forrester.

'Nothing on earth,' said Mrs Thorne. 'She is my special friend and is in my opinion a great deal more than worthy of my Uncle Francis. Only papa who dislikes them both would like to make it out that the two of them are going to cut their own throats each by marrying the other. I wish papa could have heard the way in which she said that he would have to marry them, — unless the Bishop should like to come forward and perform the ceremony.'

'I shall do nothing of the kind,' said the Dean angrily.

'If you had heard,' continued his daughter, 'all that she had to say about the family name and the family property, and the family grandeur generally, you would have thought her the most becoming young woman in the country to be the future Lady Geraldine.'

'I wish you wouldn't talk of it, my dear,' said Mrs Hippesley.

'We shall have to talk of it, and had better become used to it among ourselves. I don't suppose that Miss Altifiorla has invented the story out of her own head. She would not say that she was engaged to marry my uncle if it were not true.'

'It's my belief,' said the Dean getting up and walking out of the room in great anger, 'that Sir Francis Geraldine will never marry Miss Altifiorla.'

'I don't think my brother will ever marry Miss Altifiorla,' said Mrs Dean. 'He is very silly and very vicious, but I don't think he'll ever do anything so bad as that.'

'Poor Miss Altifiorla,' said Mrs Thorne afterwards to her Aunt Forrester.

That same evening Miss Altifiorla, feeling that she had broken the ice, and oppressed by the weight of the secret which was a secret still in every house in Exeter except the Deanery, wrote to her other friend Mrs Green and begged her to come down. She had tidings to tell of the greatest importance. So Mrs Green put on her bonnet and came down. 'My dear,' said Miss Altifiorla, 'I have something to tell you. I am going to be —'

'Not married!' said Mrs Green.

'Yes, I am. How very odd that you should guess. But yet when I come to think of it I don't know that it is odd. Because after all there does come a time in, — a lady's life when it is probable that she will marry.' Miss Altifiorla hesitated, having in the first instance desired to use the word girl.

'That's as may be,' said Mrs Green. 'Your principles used to be on the other side.'

'Of course all that changes when the opportunity comes. It wasn't so much that I disliked the idea of marriage for myself, as that I was proud of the freedom which I enjoyed. However that is all over. I am free no longer.'

'And who is it to be?'

'Ah, who is it to be? Can you make a guess?'

'Not in the least. I don't know of anybody who has been spooning you.'

'Oh, what a term to use! No one can say that any one ever — spooned me. It is a horrible word. And I cannot bear to hear it fall from my own lips.'

'It is what young men do do,' said Mrs Green.

'That I think depends on the rank in life which the young men occupy; — and also the young women. I can understand that a Bank clerk should do it to an attorney's daughter.'

'Well; who is it you are going to marry without spooning, which in my vocabulary is simply another word for two young people being fond of each other.' Miss Altifiorla remained silent for a while, feeling that she owed it to herself to awe her present companion by her manner before she should crush her altogether by the weight of the name she would have to pronounce. Mrs Green had received her communication flippantly, and had probably felt that her friend intended to demean herself by some mere common marriage. 'Who is to be the happy swain?' asked Mrs Green.

'Swain!' said Miss Altifiorla, unable to repress her feelings.

'Well; lover, young man, suitor, husband as is to be. Some word common on such occasion will I suppose fit him.'

Miss Altifiorla felt that no word common on such occasions would fit him. But yet it was necessary that she should name him, having gone so far. And, having again been silent for a minute so as to bethink herself in what most dignified language this might be done, she proceeded. 'I am to be allied,' — again there was a little pause, — 'to Sir Francis Geraldine!'

'Him Cecilia Holt rejected!'

'Him who I think was fortunate enough to escape Cecilia Holt.'

'Goodness gracious! It seems but the other day.'

'Cecilia Holt has since recovered from her wounds and married another husband, and is now suffering from fresh wounds. Is it odd that the gentleman should have found some one else to love when the lady has had time not only to love but to marry, and to be separated from another man?'

'Sir Francis Geraldine!' ejaculated Mrs Green.

'Well; I'm sure I wish you all the joy in the world. When is it to be?' But Mrs Green had so offended Miss Altifiorla by her manner of accepting the news that she could not bring herself to make any further gracious answer. Mrs Green therefore took her leave and the fact of Miss Altifiorla's engagement was soon known all over Exeter.

Chapter XXI

LADY GRANT
AT DRESDEN

'You have first to believe the story as I tell it you,
and get out of your head altogether the story as
you have conceived it.' This was said by Lady
Grant to her brother when she had travelled all
the way to Dresden with the purpose of inducing
him to take his wife back. She had come there
solely with that object, and it must be said of her
that she had well done her duty as a sister. But she
found it by no means easy to induce her brother to
look at the matter with her eyes. In fact, it was evident to her that he did not believe the story as she
had told it. She must go on and din it into his ears
till by perseverance she should change his belief.
He still thought that credit should be given to that
letter from Sir Francis, although he was aware
that to Sir Francis himself as a man he would have
given no credit whatsoever. It had suited his suspicions to believe that there had been something
in common between Sir Francis and his wife up to
the moment in which the terrible fact of her engagement had been made known to him; and
from that belief he could not free his mind. He
had already been persuaded to say that she should
come back to him, — but she should come as a
sinner confessing her sin. He would take her back,
but as one whom he had been justified in expel-

ling, and to whom he should be held as extending great mercy.

But Lady Grant would not accept of his mercy, nor would she encourage her coming back with such a purpose. It would not be good in the first place for him that he should think that his wife had been an offender. His future happiness must depend on his fixed belief in her purity and truth. And, as for her, — Lady Grant was sure that no entreaties would induce her to own that she had been in the wrong. She desired to have no pardon asked, but would certainly ask for no pardon on her own behalf.

'Why was it that he came, then, to my house?' asked Mr Western.

'Am I, or rather is she, to account for the conduct of such a man as that? Are you to make her responsible for his behaviour?'

'She was engaged to him.'

'Undoubtedly. It should have been told to you, — though I can understand the reasons which kept her silent from day to day. The time will come when you will understand it also, and know, as I do, how gracious and how feminine has been her silence.' Then there came across her brother's face a look of doubt as indicating his feeling that nothing could have justified her silence. 'Yes, George; the time will come that you will understand her altogether although you are far from doing so now.'

'I believe you think her to be perfect,' said he.

'Hardly perfect, because she is a human being.

But although I know her virtues I have not known her faults. It may be that she is too proud, — a little unwilling, perhaps, to bend. Most women will bend whether they be in fault or not. But would you wish your wife to do so?'

'I, at any rate, have not asked her.'

'You, at any rate, have not given her the opportunity. My accusation against you is, that you sent her away from you on an accusation made solely by that man, and without waiting to hear from herself whether she would plead guilty to it.'

'I deny it.'

'Yes; I hear your denial. But you will have to acknowledge it, at any rate to yourself, before you can ever hope to be a happy man.'

'When he wrote to me, I believed the whole story to be a lie from first to last.'

'And when you found that it was not all a lie, then it became to you a gospel throughout. You could not understand that the very faults which had induced her to break her engagement were of a nature to make him tell his story untruly.'

'When she acknowledged herself to have been engaged to him it nearly broke my heart.'

'Just so. And with your heart broken you would not sift the truth. She had committed no offense against you in engaging herself.'

'She should have told me as soon as we knew each other.'

'She should have told you before she accepted your offer. But she had been deterred from doing so by your own revelation to her. You cannot believe that she intended you always to be in the dark. You cannot imagine that she had expected that you should never hear of her adventure with Sir Francis Geraldine.'

'I do not know.'

'I had heard it, and she knew that I had heard it.'

'Why did you not tell me, then?'

'Do you suppose that I wished to interfere between you and your wife? Of course I told her that you ought to know. Of course I told her that you ought to have known it already. But she excused herself, — with great sorrow. Things had presented themselves in such a way that the desired opportunity of telling you had never come.' He shook his head. 'I tell you that it was so, and you are bound to believe it of one of whom in all other respects you had thought well; of one who loved you with the fondest devotion. Instead of that there came this man with his insidious falsehoods, with his implied lies; this man, of whom you have always thought so badly; — and him you believed instead! I tell you that you can justify yourself before no human being. You were not entitled to repudiate your wife for such offence as she had committed, you are not entitled even had there been no mutual affection to bind you together. How much less so in your present condition, — and in hers. People will only excuse you by saying that you were mad. And now in order to put yourself right, you expect that she shall come forward, and own herself to have been the cause of this break. I tell you that she will not do it. I would not even ask her to do it; — not for her sake, nor for your own.'

'I am then to go,' said he, 'and grovel in the dust before her feet.'

'There need be no grovelling. There need be no confessions.'

'How then?'

'Go to Exeter, and simply take her. Disregard what all the world may say for the sake of her happiness and for your own. She will make no stipulation. She will simply throw herself into your arms with unaffected love. Do not let her have to undergo the suffering of bringing forth your child without the comfort of knowing that you are near to her.' Then she left him to think in solitude over the words she had spoken to him.

He did think of them. But he found it to be impossible to put absolute faith in them. It was not that he thought that his sister was deceiving him, that he distrusted her who had taken this long journey at great personal trouble altogether on his behalf; but that he could not bring himself to believe that he himself had been so cruel as to reject his young wife without adequate cause. It had gradually come across his mind that he had been most cruel, most unjust, — if he had done so; and to this judgment, passed by himself on himself, he would not submit. In concealing her engagement she had been very wrong, but it must be that she had concealed more than her engagement. And to have been engaged to such a man added much to the fault in his estimation. He would not acknowledge that she had been deceived as to the man's character and had set herself right before it was too late. Why had the man come to his house and asked for him, — after what had passed between them, — if not in compliance with some understanding between him and her? But yet he would take her back if she would confess her fault and beg his pardon, — for then he would be saved the disgrace of having to acknowledge that he had been in fault from the first.

His sister left him alone without saying a word on the subject for twenty-four hours, and then again attacked him. 'George,' she said, 'I must go back to-morrow. I have left my children all alone and cannot stay longer away from them.'

'Must you go to-morrow?' he asked.

'Indeed, yes. Had not the matter been one of almost more than life and death I should not have come. Am I to return and feel that my journey has been for nothing?'

'What would you have me do?'

'Return with me, and go at once to Exeter.'

He almost tore his hair in his agony as he walked about the room before he replied to her. But she remained silent, watching him. 'You must leave me here till I think about it.'

'Then I might as well not have come at all,' she said.

He moved about the room in an agony of

spirit. He knew it to be essential to his future happiness in life that he should be the master in his own house. And he felt that he could not be so unless he should be known to have been right in this terrible misfortune with which their married life had been commenced. There was no obliterating it, no forgetting it, no ignoring it. He had in his passion gone away from her, and passionately, she had withdrawn. Let them not say a word about it, there would still have been this terrible event in both their memories. And for himself he knew that unless it could be settled from the first that he had acted with justice, his life would be intolerable to him. He was a man, and it behoved him to have been just. She was a woman, and the feeling of having had to be forgiven would not be so severe with her. She, when taken a second time into grace and pardoned, might still rejoice and be happy. But for himself, he reminded himself over and over again that he was a man, and assured himself that he could never lift up his head were he by his silence to admit that he had been in the wrong.

But still his mind was changed, — was altogether changed by the coming of his sister. Till she had come all had been a blank with him, in which no light had been possible. He could see no life before him but one in which he should be constantly condemned by his fellow-men because of his cruelty to his young wife. Men would not stop to ask whether he had been right or wrong, but would declare him at any rate to have been stern and cruel. And then he had been torn to the heart by his memory of those passages of love which had been so sweet to him. He had married her to be the joy of his life, and she had become so to his entire satisfaction when in his passion he had sent her away. He already knew that he had made a great mistake. Angry as he had been, he should not have thus sought to avenge himself. He should have known himself better than to think that because she had been in fault he could therefore live without her. He had owned to himself, when his sister had come to him, that he must use her services in getting his wife once again. Was she not the one human being that suited him at all points? But still, — but still his honour must be saved. If she in truth desired to come back to him, she would not hesitate to own that she had been in fault.

'What am I to say to her? What message will you send to her? You will hardly let me go back without some word.' This was said to him by his sister as he walked about the room in his misery. What message could he send? He desired to return himself, and was willing to do so at a moment's notice if only he could be assured that if he did so she would as a wife do her duty by owning that she had been in the wrong. How should he live with a wife who would always be asserting to herself, and able to assert to him, that in this extremity of their trouble he had been the cause of it, — not that she would so assert it aloud, but that the power of doing so would be always present to her and to him? And yet he was resolved to return, and if he allowed his sister to go back without him never would there come so fair an opportunity again. 'I have done my duty by you,' said his sister.

'Yes, yes. I need hardly tell you that I am grateful to you.'

'And now do your duty by her.'

'If she will write to me one line to beg me to come I will do so.'

'You have absolutely driven her away from you, and left her abruptly, so that she should have no opportunity of imploring you to spare her. And now you expect that she should do so?'

'Yes; — if she were wrong. By your own showing she was the first to sin against me.'

'You do not know the nature of a woman, and especially you do not know hers. I have nothing further to say. I shall leave this by the early train to-morrow morning, and you can go with me or let me go alone as you please. I have said what I came to say, and if I have said it without effect it will only show me how hard a man's heart may become by living in the world.' Then she left him alone and went her way.

He took his hat and escaped from the Hotel and walked along the Elbe all alone. He went far down the river, and did not return for many hours. At first his thoughts were full of anger against his sister, though he acknowledged that she had taken great trouble in coming there on a mission intended to be beneficent to them both.

With the view solely of doing her duty to her brother and to her sister-in-law, she had taken infinite trouble. Yet he was very angry with her. Being a woman she had most unjustly taken the part of another woman against him. Cecilia would have suffered but little in having been forced to acknowledge her great sin. But he would suffer greatly, — he who had sinned not at all, — by the tacit confession which he would be thus compelled to make. It was true that it was necessary that he should return. The happiness of them all, including that unborn child, required it. His sister, knowing this, demanded that he should sacrifice himself in order that his wife might be indulged in her pride. And yet he knew that he must do it. Though he might go to her in silence, and in silence renew his married life, he would by so doing confess that he had been wrong. To such confession he should not be driven. In the very gall of bitterness, and with the sense of injustice strong upon him, he did resolve that he would return to England with his sister. But having so resolved, with his wrath hot against Lady Grant, his mind gradually turned to Cecilia and her condition. How sweet would it be to have her once again sitting at his table, once again leaning on his arm, once again looking up into his face with almost comical doubt, seeking to find in his eyes what answer he would best like her to make when referring to her for some decision. 'It is your opinion that I want,' he would say. 'Ah! but if I only knew yours I should be so much better able to have one of my own.' Then there would come a look over her face which almost maddened him when he thought that he should never see it again. It was the idea that she who could so look at him should have looked with the same smile into the face of that other man which had driven him to fury; — that she should have so looked in those very days in which she had gazed into his own.

Could it be that though she had been engaged to the man she had never taken delight in so gazing at him? That girl whom he had thought to make his wife, and who had so openly jilted him, had never understood him as Cecilia had done, — had never looked at him as Cecilia had looked. But he, after he had been so treated, — happily so treated, — had certainly never desired to see the girl. But this wife of his, who was possessed of all the charms which a woman could own, of whom he acknowledged to himself day after day that she was, as regarded his taste, peerless and unequalled, she after breaking from that man, that man unworthy to be called a gentleman, still continued to hold intercourse with him! Was it not clear that she had still remained on terms of intimacy with him?

His walk along the Elbe was very bitter, but yet he determined to return to England with his sister.

Chapter XXII

MR WESTERN
YIELDS

The fact that Lady Grant had gone to Dresden was not long in reaching the ears of Mrs Western. Dick Ross had heard at the club of Perth that she had gone and had told Sir Francis. Sir Francis passed on the news to Miss Altifiorla, and from her it had reached the deserted wife. Miss Altifiorla had not told it direct because at that time she and Cecilia were not supposed to be on friendly terms. But the tidings had got about and Mrs Western had heard them.

'She's a good woman,' said Cecilia to her mother. 'I knew her to be that the first moment that she came to me. She is rough as he is, and stern, and has a will of her own. But her heart is tender and true; — as is his also at the core.'

'I don't know about that,' said Mrs Holt, with the angry tone which she allowed herself to use only when speaking of Mr Western.

'Yes, he is, mamma. In your affection for me you will not allow yourself to be just to him. In truth you hardly know him.'

'I know that he has destroyed your happiness for ever, and made me very wretched.'

'No, mamma; not for ever. It may be that he will come for me, and that then we shall be as happy as the day is long.' As she said this a vision came before her eyes of the birth of her child and of her surroundings at the time; — the anxious solicitude of a loving husband, the care of attendants who would be happy because she was happy, the congratulations of friends, and the smiles of the world. But above all she pictured to herself her husband standing by her bedside with the child in his arms. The dream had been dreamed before, and was re-dreamed during every hour of the day. 'Lady Grant is strong,' she continued, 'and can plead for me better than I could plead myself.'

'Plead for you! Why should there be any one wanted to plead for you? Will Lady Grant plead with you for her brother?'

'It is not necessary. My own heart pleads for him. It is because he has been in the wrong that an intercessor is necessary for me. It is they who commit the injury that have a difficulty in forgiving. If he came to me do you not know that I should throw myself into his arms and be the happiest woman in the world without a word spoken?' The conversation was not then carried further, but Mrs Holt continued to shake her head as she sat at her knitting. In her estimation no husband could have behaved worse than had her son-in-law. And she was of opinion that he should be punished for his misconduct before things could be made smooth again.

Some days afterwards Miss Altifiorla called at the house and sent in a note while she stood waiting in the hall. In the note she merely asked whether her dear 'Cecilia' would be willing to receive her after what had passed. She had news to tell of much importance, and she hoped that her 'dear Cecilia' would receive her. There had been no absolute quarrel, no quarrel known to the servants, and Cecilia did receive her. 'Oh, my dear,' she said, bursting into the room with an air of affected importance, 'you will be surprised, — I think that you must be surprised at what I have to tell you.'

'I will be surprised if you wish it,' said Cecilia.

'Let me first begin by assuring you, that you must not make light of my news. It is of the greatest importance, not only to me, but of some importance also to you.'

'It shall be of importance.'

'Because you begin with that little sneer which has become so common with you. You must be aware of it. Amidst the troubles of your own life, which we all admit to be very grievous, there has come upon you a way of thinking that no one else's affairs can be of any importance.'

'I am not aware of it.'

'It is so a little. And pray believe me that I am not in the least angry about it. I knew that it would be so when I came to you this morning; and yet I could not help coming. Indeed as the thing has now been made known to the Dean's family I could not bear that you should be left any longer in ignorance.'

'What is the thing?'

'There it is again; — that sneer. I cannot tell

you unless you will interest yourself. Does nothing interest you now beyond your own misfortunes?'

'Alas, no. I fear not.'

'But this shall interest you. You must be awaked to the affairs of the world, — especially such an affair as this. You must be shaken up. This I suppose will shake you up. If not, you must be past all hope.'

'What on earth is it?'

'Sir Francis Geraldine — ! You have heard at any rate of Sir Francis Geraldine.'

'Well, yes; I have not as yet forgotten the name.'

'I should think not. Sir Francis Geraldine has —' And then she paused again.

'Cut his little finger,' said Cecilia. Had she dreamed of what was to come she would not have turned Sir Francis into ridicule. But she had been aware of Miss Altifiorla's friendship with Sir Francis, — or rather what she had regarded as an affectation of friendship, and did not for a moment anticipate such a communication as was to be made to her.

'Cecilia Holt —'

'That at any rate is not my name.'

'I dare say you wish it were.'

'I would not change my real name for that of any woman under the sun.'

'Perhaps not; — but there are other women in a position of less grandeur. I am going to change mine.'

'No!'

'I thought you would be surprised because it would look as though I were about to abandon my great doctrine. It is not so. My opinions on that great subject are not in the least changed. But of course there must be some women whom the exigencies of the world will require to marry.'

'A good many, first and last.'

'About the good many I am not at this moment concerning myself. My duty is clearly before me and I mean to perform it. I have been asked to ally myself —'; then there was a pause, and the speaker discovered when it was too late that she was verging on the ridiculous in declaring her purpose of forming an alliance; — 'that is to say, I am going to marry Sir Francis.'

'Sir Francis Geraldine!'

'Do you see any just cause or impediment?'

'None in the least. And yet how am I to answer such a question? I saw cause or impediment why I should not marry him.'

'You both saw it, I suppose?' said Miss Altifiorla, with an air of grandeur. 'You both supposed that you were not made for each other, and wisely determined to give up the idea. You did not remain single, and I suppose we need not either.'

'Certainly not for my sake.'

'Our intimacy since that time has been increased by circumstances, and we have now discovered that we can both of us best suit our own interests by an —'

'An alliance,' suggested Mrs Western.

'If you please, — though I am quite aware that you use the term as a sneer.' As to this Mrs Western was too honest to deny the truth, and remained silent.

'I thought it proper,' continued Miss Altifiorla, 'as we had been so long friends, to inform you that it will be so. You had your chance, and as you let it slip I trust that you will not envy me mine.'

'Not in the least.'

'At any rate you do not congratulate me.'

'I have been very remiss. I acknowledge it. But upon my word the news has so startled me that I have been unable to remember the common courtesies of the world. I thought when I heard of your travelling up to London together that you were becoming very intimate.'

'Oh, it had been ever so much before that, — the intimacy at least. Of course I did not know him before he came to this house. But a great many things have happened since that; — have there not? Well, good-bye, dear. I have no doubt we shall continue as friends, especially as we shall be living almost in the neighbourhood. Castle Gerald is to be at once fitted up for me, and I hope you will forget all our little tiffs, and often come and stay with me.' So saying, Miss Altifiorla, having told her grand news, made her adieus and went away.

'A great many things have happened since that,' said Cecilia, repeating to herself her

friend's words. It seemed to her to be so many that a lifetime had been wasted since Sir Francis had first come to that house. She had won the love of the best man she had ever known, and married him, and had then lost his love! And now she had been left as a widowed wife, with all the coming troubles of maternity on her head. She had understood well the ill-natured sarcasm of Miss Altifiorla. 'We shall be living almost in the same neighbourhood!' Yes; if her separation from her husband was to be continued, then undoubtedly she would live at Exeter, and, as far as the limits of the county were concerned, she would be the neighbour of the future Lady Geraldine. That she should ever willingly be found under the same roof with Sir Francis was, as she knew well, as impossible to Miss Altifiorla as to herself. The invitation contained the sneer, and was intended to contain it. But it created no anger. She, too, had sneered at Miss Altifiorla quite as bitterly. They had each learned to despise the other, and not to sneer was impossible. Miss Altifiorla had come to tell of her triumph, and to sneer in return. But it mattered nothing. What did matter was whether that threat should come true. Should she always be left living at Exeter with her mother? Then she dreamed her dream again, — that he had come back to her, and was sitting by her bedside with his hand in hers and whispering sweet words to her, while a baby was lying in her arms — his child. As she thought of the bliss of the fancied moment, the still possible bliss, her anger seemed to fade away. What would she not do to bring him back, what would she not say? She had done amiss in keeping that secret so long, and though the punishment had been severe, it was not altogether undeserved. It had come to him as a terrible blow, and he had been unable to suppress his agony. He should not have treated her so; no, he should not have sent her away. But she could make excuses now which but a few weeks since seemed to her to be impossible. And she understood, — she told herself that she understood, — the difference between herself as a woman and him as a man. He had a right to command, a right to be obeyed, a right to be master. He had a right to know all the secrets of her heart, and to be offended when one so important had been kept from him. He had lifted his hand in great wrath, and the blow he had struck had been awful. But she would bear it without a word of complaint if only he would come back to her. As she thought of it, she declared to herself that she must die if he did not come back. To live as she was living now would be impossible to her. But if he would come back, how absolutely would she disregard all that the world might say as to their short quarrel. It would indeed be known to all the world, but what could the world do to her if she once again had her husband by her side? When the blow first fell on her she had thought much of the ignominy which had befallen her, and which must ever rest with her. Even though she should be taken back again, people would know that she had been discarded. But now she told herself that for that she cared not at all. Then she again dreamed her dream. Her child was born, and her husband was standing by her with that sweet manly smile upon his face. She put out her hand as though he would touch it, and was conscious of an involuntary movement as though she were bending her face towards him for a kiss.

Surely he would come to her! His sister had gone to him, and would have told him the absolute truth. She had never sinned against him, even by intentional silence. There had been no thought of hers since she had been his wife which he had not been welcome to share. It had in truth been for his sake rather than for her own that she had been silent. She was aware that from cowardice her silence had been prolonged. But surely now at last he would forgive her that offense. Then she thought of the words she would use as she owned her fault. He was a man, and as a man had a right to expect that she would confess it. If he would come to her, and stand once again with his arm round her waist, she would confess it.

'My dear, here is a letter. The postman has just brought it.' She took the letter from her mother's hand and hardly knew whether to be pleased or disappointed when she found that the address was in the handwriting of Lady Grant. Lady Grant would of course write whether with good news or with bad. The address told her nothing, but yet she could not tear the envelope. 'Well, my dear; what is it?' said her mother. 'Why don't you open it?'

She turned a soft supplicating painful look up to her mother's face as she begged for grace. 'I will go up-stairs, mamma, and will tell you by and by.' Then she left the room with the letter unopened in her hand. It was with difficulty that she could examine its contents, so apprehensive was she and yet so hopeful, so confident at one moment of her coming happiness, and yet so fearful at another that she should be again enveloped in the darkness of her misery. But she did at last persuade herself to read the words which Lady Grant had written. They were very short, and ran as follows; 'MY DEAR CECILIA, my brother returns with me, and will at once go down to Exeter.' The shock of her joy was so great that she could hardly see what followed. 'He will hope to reach that place on the fifteenth by the train which leaves London at nine in the morning.'

That was all, but that was enough. She was sure that he would not come with the purpose of telling her that he must again leave her. And she was sure also that if he would once put himself within the sphere of her personal influence it should be so used that he would never leave her again.

'Of course he is coming. I knew he would come. Why should he not come?' This she exclaimed to her mother, and then went on to speak of him with a wild rhapsody of joy, as though there had hardly been any breach in her happiness. And she continued to sing the praises of her husband till Mrs Holt hardly knew how to bear her enthusiasm in a fitting mood. For she, who was not in love, still thought that this man's conduct had been scandalous, wicked and cruel; and, if to be forgiven, only to be forgiven because of the general wickedness and cruelty of man. But she was not allowed to say a word not in praise; and, because she could not in truth praise him, was scolded as though she was anxious to rob her daughter of her joys.

It had not been without great difficulty that Lady Grant induced her brother to assent to her writing the letter which has been given above. When he had agreed to return with her to England he had no doubt assented to her assertion that he was bound to take his wife back again, even without any confession. And this had been so much to gain, had been so felt to be the one only material point necessary, that he was not pressed as to his manner of doing it. But before they reached London it was essential that some arrangement should be made for bringing them together. 'Could not I go down to Durton,' he had said, 'and could not she come to me there?' No doubt he might have gone to Durton, and no doubt she would have gone to him if asked. She would have flown to him at Dresden, or to Jerusalem, at a word spoken by him. Absence had made him so precious to her, that she would have obeyed the slightest behest with joy as long as the order given were to bring them once more together. But of this Lady Grant was not aware, and, had she been so, the sense of what was becoming would have restrained her.

'I think, George, that you had better go to Exeter,' she said.

'Should we not be more comfortable at Durton?'

'I think that when at Durton you will be more happy if you shall yourself have fetched her from her mother's home. I think you owe it to your wife to go to her, and make the journey with her. What is your objection?'

'I do not wish to be seen in Exeter,' he replied.

'Nor did she you may be sure when she returned there alone. But what does it matter? If you can be happy in once more possessing her, it cannot signify who shall see you. There can be nothing to be ashamed of in going for your wife; nor can any evil happen to you. As this thing is to be done, let it be done in a noble spirit.'

Then the letter as above given was written.

Chapter XXIII

SIR FRANCIS' ESCAPE

When she had told the Dean's family, and Mrs Green, and Cecilia, Miss Altifiorla began to feel that there was no longer a secret worth the keeping. And indeed it became necessary to her happiness to divulge this great step in life which she was about to take. She had written very freely, and very frequently to Sir Francis, and Sir Francis, to tell the truth, had not responded in the same spirit. She had received but two answers to six letters, and each answer had been conveyed in about three lines. There had been no expressions from him of confiding love nor any pressing demands for an immediate marriage. They had all been commenced without even naming her, and had been finished by the simple signature of his initials. But to Miss Altifiorla they had been satisfactory. She knew how silly she would be to expect from such an one as her intended husband long epistles such as a school girl would require, and, in order to keep him true to her, had determined to let him know how little exacting she was inclined to be. She would willingly do all the preliminary writing if only she could secure her position as Lady Geraldine. She wrote such letters, letters so full of mingled wit and love and fun, that she was sure that he must take delight in reading

273

them. 'Easy reading requires hard writing,' she said to herself as she copied for the third time one of her epistles, and copied it studiously in such handwriting that it should look to have been the very work of negligence. In all this she had been successful as she thought, and told herself over and over again how easy it was for a clever woman to make captive a man of mark, provided that she set herself assiduously to the task.

She soon descended from her friends to the shopkeepers, and found that her news was received very graciously by the mercantile interests of the city. The milliners, the haberdashers, the furriers and the bootmakers of Exeter received her communication and her orders with pleased alacrity. With each of them she held a little secret conference, telling each with a smiling whisper what fate was about to do for her. To even the upholsterers, the bankers, the hotel-keepers and the owners of post-horses she was communicative, making every one the gratified recipient of her tidings. Thus in a short time all Exeter knew that Sir Francis Geraldine was about to lead to the hymeneal altar Miss Altifiorla, and it must be acknowledged that all Exeter expressed various opinions on the subject. They who understood that Miss Altifiorla was to pay for the supplies ordered out of her own pocket declared for the most part how happy a man was Sir Francis. But those who could only look to Sir Francis for possible future custom were surprised that the Baronet should have allowed himself to be so easily caught. And then the aristocracy expressed its opinion, which it must be acknowledged was for the most part hostile to Miss Altifiorla. It was well known through the city that the Dean had declared that he would never again see his brother-in-law at the Deanery. And it was whispered that the Reverend Dr Pigrum, one of the canons, had stated 'that no one in the least knew where Miss Altifiorla had come from.' This hit Miss Altifiorla very hard, — so much so that she felt herself obliged to write an indignant letter to Dr Pigrum, giving at length her entire pedigree. To this Dr Pigrum made a reply as follows. 'Dr Pigrum's compliments to Miss Altifiorla and is happy to learn the name of her great grandmother.' Dr Pigrum was supposed to be a wag and the letter soon became the joint property of all the ladies in the Close.

This interfered much with Miss Altifiorla's happiness. She even went across to Cecilia complaining of the great injustice done to her by the Cathedral clergymen generally. 'Men from whom one should expect charity instead of scandal, but that their provincial ignorance is so narrow!' Then she went on to remind Cecilia how much older was the Roman branch of her family than even the blood of the Geraldines. 'You oughtn't to have talked about it,' said Cecilia, who in her present state of joy did not much mind Miss Altifiorla and her husband. 'Do you suppose that I intend to be married under a bushel?' said Miss Altifiorla grandly.

But there appeared a paragraph in the *Western Telegraph* which drove Miss Altifiorla nearly mad. 'It is understood that one of the aristocracy in this county is soon about to be married to a lady who has long lived among us in Exeter. Sir Francis Geraldine is the happy man, and Miss Altifiorla is the lady about to become Lady Geraldine. Miss Altifiorla is descended from an Italian family of considerable note in its own country. Her great grandmother was a Fiasco, and her great great grandmother a Disgrazia. We are delighted to find that Sir Francis is to ally himself to a lady of such high birth.' Now Miss Altifiorla was well aware that there was an old feud between Sir Francis and the *Western Telegraph*, and she observed also that the paper made allusion to the very same relatives whom she had named in her unfortunate letter to Dr Pigrum. 'The vulgarity of the people of this town is quite unbearable,' she exclaimed to Mrs Green. But when left alone she at once wrote a funnier letter than ever to Sir Francis. It might be that Sir Francis should not see the paragraph. At any rate she did not mention it.

But unfortunately Sir Francis did see the paragraph; and, unfortunately also, he had not appreciated the wit of Miss Altifiorla's letters. 'Oh, laws!' he had been heard to ejaculate on receipt of a former letter.

'It's the kind of thing a man has to put up with when he gets married,' said Captain McCollop, a gentleman who had already in some sort succeeded Dick Ross.

'I don't suppose you think a man ever ought to be married.'

'Quite the contrary. When a man has a property he must be married. I suppose I shall have the McCollop acres some of these days myself.' The McCollop acres were said to lie somewhere in Caithness, but no one knew their exact locality. 'But a man will naturally put off the evil day as long as he can. I should have thought that you might have allowed yourself to run another five years yet.' The flattery did touch Sir Francis, and he began to ask himself whether he had gone too far with Miss Altifiorla. Then came the *Western Telegraph* and he told himself that he had not gone too far.

'Good Heavens! she has told everybody in that beastly hole,' said he. The 'beastly hole' was intended to represent Exeter.

'Of course she has. You didn't suppose but that she would begin to wear her honour and glory as soon as they were wearable.'

'She pledged herself not to mention it to a single soul,' said Sir Francis. Upon this Captain McCollop merely shrugged his shoulders. 'I'll be whipped if I put up with it. Look here! All her filthy progenitors put into the newspaper to show how grand she is.'

'I shouldn't care so very much about that,' said the cautious Captain, who began to perceive that he need not be specially bitter against the lady.

'You're not going to marry her.'

'Well; no; that's true.'

'Nor am I,' said Sir Francis with an air of great decision. 'She hasn't got a word of mine in writing to show, — not a word that would go for anything with a jury.'

'Hasn't she indeed?'

'Not a word. I have taken precious good care of that. Between you and me I don't mind acknowledging it. But it had never come to more than that.'

'Then in fact you are not bound to her.'

'No; I am not; — not what I call bound. She's a handsome woman you know, — very handsome.'

'I suppose so.'

'And she'd do the drawing-room well, and the sitting at the top of the table, and all that kind of thing.'

'But it's such a heavy price to pay,' said Captain McCollop.

'I should not have minded the price,' said Sir Francis, not quite understanding his friend's remark, 'if she hadn't made me ridiculous in this way. The Fiascos and the Disgrazias! What are they to our old English families? If she had let it remain as it was I might have gone through with it. But as she has told all Exeter and got that stuff put into the newspapers, she must take the consequences. One is worse than another, as far as I can see.' By this Sir Francis intended to express his opinion that Miss Altifiorla was at any rate quite as bad as Cecilia Holt.

But the next thing to be decided was the mode of escape. Though Sir Francis had declared that he was not what he called bound, yet he knew that he must take some steps in the matter to show that he considered himself to be free, and as the Captain was a clever man, and well conversant with such things, he was consulted. 'I should say, take a run abroad for a short time,' said the Captain.

'Is that necessary?'

'You'd avoid some of the disagreeables. People will talk, and your relatives at Exeter might kick up a row.'

'Never mind my relatives.'

'With all my heart. But people have such a way of making themselves disgusting. What do you say to taking a run through the States?'

'Would you go with me?' asked the Baronet.

'If you wish it I shouldn't mind,' said the Captain considerately. 'Only to do any good we should be off quickly. But you must write to someone first.'

'Before I start, you think?'

'Oh, yes; — certainly. If she didn't hear from you before you went you'd be persecuted by her letters.'

'There is no end to her letters. I've quite made up my mind what I'll do about them. I won't open one of them. After all why should she write to me when the affair is over? You've heard of Mrs Western I suppose?'

'Yes; I've heard of her.'

'I didn't write to her when that affair was over. I didn't pester her with long-winded scrawls. She changed her mind, and I've changed mine; and so we're equal. I've paid her and she can pay me if she knows how.'

'I hope Miss Altifiorla will look at it in the same light,' said the Captain.

'Why shouldn't she? She knew all about it when that other affair came to an end. I wasn't treated with any particular ceremony. The truth is people don't look at these things now as they used to do. Men and women mostly do as they like till they've absolutely fixed themselves. There used to be duels and all that kind of nonsense. There is none of that now.'

'No; you won't get shot.'

'I don't mind being shot any more than another man; but you must take the world as you find it. One young woman treated me awfully rough, to tell the truth. And why am I not to treat another just as roughly? If you look at it all round you'll see that I have used them just as they have used me.'

'At any rate,' said Captain McCollop after a pause, 'if you have made up your mind, you'd better write the letter.'

Sir Francis did not see the expediency of writing the letter immediately, but at last he gave way to his friend's arguments. And he did so the more readily as his friend was there to write the letter for him. After some attempts on his own part, he put the writing of the letter into the hands of the Captain, and left him alone for an entire morning to perform the task. The letter when it was sent, after many corrections and revises, ran as follows,

'My Dear Miss Altifiorla,
'I think that I am bound in honour without a moment's delay to make you aware of the condition of my mind in regard to marriage. I ain't quite sure but what I shall be better without it altogether.'

— 'I'd rather marry her twice over than let my cousin have the title and the property,' said the Baronet with energy. 'You needn't tell her that,' said McCollop. 'Of course when you've cleared the ground in this quarter you can begin again with another lady.' —

'I think that perhaps I may have expressed myself badly so as to warrant you in understanding more than I have meant. If so I am sure the fault has been mine, and I am very sorry for it. Things have turned up with which I need not perhaps trouble you, and compel me to go for a while to a very distant country. I shall be off almost before I can receive a reply to this letter. Indeed I may be gone before an answer can reach me. But I have thought it right not to let a post go by without informing you of my decision.

'I have seen that article in the Exeter news-paper respecting your family in Italy, and think that it must be very gratifying to you. I did understand, however, that not a word was to have been spoken as to the matter. Nothing had escaped from me at any rate. I fear that some of your intimate friends at Exeter must have been indiscreet.

'Believe me yours,

'With the most sincere admiration,
'FRANCIS GERALDINE.'

He was not able to start for America immediately after writing this, but he quitted his lodge in Scotland, leaving no immediate address, and hid himself for a while among his London clubs, where he trusted that the lady might not find him. In a week's time he would be off to the United States.

Who shall picture the rage of Miss Altifiorla when she received this letter? This was the very danger which she had feared, but had hardly thought it worth her while to fear. It was the one possible break-down in her triumph; but had been, she thought, so unlikely as to be hardly possible. But now on reading the letter she felt that no redress was within her reach. To whom should she go for succour? Though her ancestors had been so noble, she had no one near her to take up the cudgels on her behalf. With her friends in Exeter she had become a little proud of late, so that she had turned from her those who might have assisted her. 'The coward!' she said to herself, 'the base coward! He dares to treat me in this way because he knows that I am alone.' Then she became angry in her heart against Cecilia, who she felt had set a dangerous example in this practice of jilting. Had Cecilia not treated Sir Francis so unceremoniously he certainly would not have dared so to treat her. There was truth in this, as in that case Sir Francis would at this moment have been the husband of Mrs Western.

But what should she do? She took out every scrap of letter that she had received from the man, and read each scrap with the greatest care. In the one letter there certainly was an offer very plainly made, as he had intended it; but she doubted whether she could depend upon it in a court of law. 'Don't you think that you and I know each other well enough to make a match of it?' It was certainly written as an offer, and her two answers to him would make it plain that it was so. But she had an idea that she would not be allowed to use her own letters against him. And then to have her gushing words read as a reply to so cold a proposition would be death to her. There was not another syllable in the whole correspondence written by him to signify that he had in truth intended to become her husband. She felt sure that he had been wickedly crafty in the whole matter, and had lured her on to expose herself in her innocence.

But what should she do? Should she write to

him an epistle full of tenderness? She felt sure that it would be altogether ineffectual. Should she fill sheets with indignation? It would be of no use unless she could follow up her indignation by strong measures. Should she let the thing pass by in silence, as though she and Sir Francis had never known each other? She could certainly do so, but that she had allowed her matrimonial prospects to become common through all Exeter. She must also let Exeter know how badly Sir Francis intended to treat her. To her too the idea of a prolonged sojourn in the United States presented itself. In former days there had come upon her a great longing to lecture at Chicago, at Saint Paul's, and at Omaha, on the distinctive duties of the female sex. Now again the idea returned to her. She thought that in one of those large Western Halls, full of gas and intelligence, she could rise to the height of her subject with a tremendous eloquence. But then would not the name of Sir Francis travel with her and crush her?

She did resolve upon informing Mrs Green. She took three days to think of it and then she sent for Mrs Green. 'Of all human beings,' she said, 'you I think are the truest to me.' Mrs Green of course expressed herself as much flattered. 'And therefore I will tell you. No false pride shall operate with me to make me hold my tongue. Of all the false deceivers that have ever broken a woman's heart that man is the basest and the falsest.'

In this way she let all Exeter know that she was not to be married to Sir Francis Geraldine; and another paragraph appeared in the *Western Telegraph*, declaring that after all Sir Francis Geraldine was not to be allied to the Fiascos and Disgrazias of Rome.

Chapter XXIV

CONCLUSION

Though the news of Miss Altifiorla's broken engagement did reach Mrs Western at St David's, she was in a state of mind which prevented her almost from recognising the fact. It was the very day on which her husband was to come to her. And her joy was so extreme as almost to have become painful. 'Mamma,' she said, 'I shall not know what to say to him.'

'Just let him come, and receive him quietly.'

'Receive him quietly! How can I be quiet when he will have come back to me? I think you do not realise the condition I have been in during the last three months.'

'Yes, my dear, I do. You have been deserted, and it has been very bad.'

But Mrs Western did not approve of the word used, as it carried a strong reproach against her husband. She was anxious now to take upon herself the whole weight of the fault which had produced their separation and to hold him to have been altogether sinless. And as yet, she was not quite sure that he would again take her to his home. All she knew was that he would be that day in Exeter and that then so much might depend on her own conduct! Of this she was quite sure, — that were he to reject her she must die. In her present condition, and with the memory present to her of the dreams she had dreamed, she could not live alone at Exeter, divided from him, and there give birth to her child. But he must surely intend to take her into his arms when he should arrive. It could not be possible that he should again reject her when he had once seen her.

Then she became fidgety about her personal appearance, — a female frailty which had never much prevailed with her, — and was anxious even about her ribbons and her dress. 'He does think so much about a woman being neat,' she said to her mother.

'I never perceived it in him, my dear.'

'Because you have not known him as I have done. He does not say much, but no one's eye is so accurate, and so severe.' All this arose from a certain passage which dwelt in her remembrance, when he had praised the fit of her gown and had told her with a kiss that no woman ever dressed so well as she did.

'I think, my dear,' continued Mrs Holt, 'that if you wear your black silk just simply, it will do very well.'

Simply! Yes; she must certainly be simple. But it is so hard to be simple in such a way as to please a man's eye. And yet, even when the time came near, she did not dare to remain long in her bedroom lest her own maid should know the source of her anxiety. At one time she had declared that she would go down to the station to meet him, but that idea had been soon abandoned. The first kiss she would give him should not be seen by strangers.

But if she were perplexed as to how she would bear herself on the coming occasion he was much more so. It may be said of him that through his whole journey home from Dresden he was disturbed, unhappy and silent; and that when his sister left him in London, and he had nothing immediately before him but the journey down to Exeter, he was almost overwhelmed by the difficulties of the situation. His case as a man was so much worse than hers as a woman. The speaking must all be done by him, and what was there that he could say? There was still present to him a keen sense of the wrong that he had endured; though he owned to himself that the punishment which at the spur of the moment he had resolved upon inflicting was too severe, — both upon her and upon himself. And though he felt that he had been injured he did gradually acknowledge that he had believed something worse than the truth. How to read the riddle he had not known, but there was a riddle which he had not read aright. If Cecilia should still be silent he must still be left in the dark. But he did understand that he was to expect no confession of a fault, and that he was to exact no show of repentance.

When the train arrived at Exeter he determined to be driven at once to the Hotel. It made him unhappy to think that every one around him should be aware that he was occupying rooms at an inn while his wife was living in the town; but he did not dare to take his portmanteau to Mrs Holt's house and hang up his hat in her hall as though nothing had been the matter. 'Put it into a cab,' he said to a porter as the door was opened, 'and bid him drive me to the Clarence.' But a man whose face he remembered had laid his hand upon his valise before it was well out of the railway carriage. 'Please, Sir,' said the man, 'you are to go up to the house and I'm to carry your things. I am Sam Barnet, the gardener.'

'Very well, Sam,' said Mr Western. 'Go on and I'll follow you.' Now, as he well knew, the house at St David's was less than half a mile from the railway station.

He felt that his misery would be over in ten minutes, and yet for ten minutes how miserable a man he was! While she was trembling with joy, a joy that was only dashed by a vague fear of his possible sternness, he was blaming his fate as it shortened by every step the distance between him and his wife. At last he had entered the path of the little garden and the door of the house was open before him. He ventured to look, but did not see her. He was in the hall, but yet he did not see her. 'Cecilia is in the breakfast parlour,' said the voice of Mrs Holt, whom in his confusion he did not notice. The breakfast parlour was in the back part of the house, looking out into the garden and thither he went. The door was just ajar and he passed in. In a second the whole trouble was over. She was in his arms at once, kissing his face, stroking his hair, leaning on his bosom, holding his arm round her own waist as though to make sure that he should not leave her; crying and laughing at the same moment. 'Oh, George, my own George! It has all been my doing; but you will forgive me! Say that one word that I am "forgiven".' Then there came another storm of kisses which frustrated the possibility of his speaking to her.

What a wife she was to possess! How graceful, how gracious, how precious were her charms, — charms in which no other woman surely ever approached her! How warm and yet how cool was the touch of her lips; how absolutely symmetrical was the sweet curve of her bust; what a fragrance came from her breath! And the light of her eyes, made more bright by her tears, shone into his with a heavenly brightness. Her soft hair as he touched it filled him with joy. And once more she was all his own. Let the secret be what it might he was quite sure that she was his own. As he bent down over her she pressed her cheek against his and again drew his arm tighter round her waist. 'George, if you wished to know how I love you, you have taken the right step. I have been sick for you, but now I shall be sick no longer. Oh, George, it was my fault; but say that you have forgiven me.'

He could not bring himself to speak so much of an accusation as would be contained in that word 'forgive'. How was he to pardon one whose present treatment to him was so perfect, so loving, and so lovely? 'Sit down, George, and let me tell you how it was. Of course I was wrong, but I did not mean to be wrong.'

'No, no,' he said. 'There shall be no wrong.' And yet why had not his sister told him that it would be like this? Why had she so stoutly maintained that Cecilia would confess nothing. Here she was acknowledging every thing with most profuse confession. What could any man desire more? 'Do not speak of it; — at any rate now. Let me be happy as I have got you.'

Then there was another storm of kisses, but she was not to be put off from her purpose. 'You must know it all. Sit down; — there, like that.' And she seated herself, leaning back upon him on the sofa. 'Before we had been abroad I had been engaged to that man.'

'Yes; — I understand that.'

'I had been engaged to him, — without knowing him. Then when I found that he was not what I thought him I made up my mind that it would be better to throw him over than make us both miserable for life.'

'Certainly.'

'And I did so. I made a struggle and did it. From that time to this I have had nothing to say to him, — nor he to me. You may say that I treated him badly.'

'I don't say so. I at any rate do not say so.'

'My own, own man. Then we went abroad and as good fortune would have it you came in our way. It was not long before you made me love you. That was not my fault, George. I loved you so dearly when you were telling me that story about the other girl; — but, somehow, I could not tell you then a similar story about myself. It seemed at first so odd that my story should be the same, and then it looked almost as though I were mocking you. Had you had no story to tell you would have known all my own before I had allowed myself to be made happy by your love. Do you not perceive that it was so?'

'Yes,' he said, slowly, 'I can understand what you mean.'

'But it was a mistake; for from day to day the difficulty grew upon me, and when once there was a difficulty I was not strong enough to overcome it. There never came the moment in which I was willing to mar my own happiness by telling you that which I thought would wound yours. I had not dreamed beforehand how much more difficult it would become when I should once be absolutely your wife. Then your sister came and she told me. She is better than anybody in the world except yourself.'

'All women are better than I am,' he said. 'It is their nature to be so.'

Some half-ludicrous idea of Miss Altifiorla and her present difficulties came across her mind, as she contradicted his assertion with another shower of kisses. 'She told me,' continued Cecilia, 'that I was bound to let you know all the truth. Of course I knew that; of course I intended it. But that odious woman was in the house and I could not tell you till she was gone. Then he came.'

'Why did he come?'

'He had no right to come. No man with the smallest spirit would have shown himself at your door. I have thought about it again and again, and I can only imagine that it had been his intention to revenge himself. But what matter his intentions so long as they do not come between you and me? I want you to know all the truth, but not to imagine more than the truth. Since the day on which I had told him that he and I must part there has been no communication between us but what you know. He came to Durton and made his way into the house, and Miss Altifiorla was there and saw it all; and then you were told.'

'He is a mean brute.'

'But I am not a brute. Am I a brute? Say that I am nice once more. You know everything now, everything, everything. I do own that I have been wrong to conceal it. My very soul should be laid bare to you.'

'Cecilia, I will never be hard to you again.'

'I do not say that you have been hard. I do not accuse you. I know that I have been wrong and I am quite content that we should again be friends. Oh, George, just at this moment I think it is sweeter than if you had never sent me away.'

And so the reconciliation was made and Mr Western and Cecilia were once more together. But no doubt, to her mind as she thought of it all, there was present the happy conviction that she had been more sinned against than sinning. She had forgiven, whereas she might have exacted forgiveness. She had been gracious, whereas she might have followed her mother's advice and have been repellent till she had brought him to her feet. As it was, her strong desire to have him once again had softened her, and now she had the double reward. She had what she wanted, and was able to congratulate herself at the same time on her virtue. But he, though he had too what he wanted, became gradually aware that he had been cruel, stiff-necked and obdurate. She was everything that he desired, but he was hardly happy because he was conscious that he had been unjust. And he was a man that loved justice even against himself, and could not be quite happy till he had made restitution.

He stayed a week with her at Exeter, during which time he so far removed himself as to be able to dine at the Deanery, and return Dr Pigrum's call. Then he was to start for his own house in Berkshire, having asked Mrs Holt to come to them a fortnight before Christmas. He would have called on Miss Altifiorla had he not understood that Miss Altifiorla in her present state of mind received no visitors. She gave it out that since men had been men and women had been women, no woman had been so basely injured as herself. But she intended to redress the wrongs of her sex by a great movement, and was devoting herself at present to hard study with that object. She used to be seen daily walking two miles and back on the Crediton Road, it being necessary to preserve her health for the sake of the great work she had in hand. But it was understood that no one was to accost her, or speak to her on these occasions, and at other times it was well known that she was engaged upon the labours of her task.

'And to-morrow we will go back to Durton,' said Mr Western to his wife.

'Dear Durton, how happy I shall be to see it once again!'

'And how happy I shall be to take you again to see it! But before we go it is necessary that I should say one thing.'

This he spoke in so stern a voice that he almost frightened her. Was it possible that after all he should find it necessary to refer again to the little fault which she had so cordially avowed?

'What is it, George?'

'I have made a mistake.'

'No, George, no, don't say so. There has been no mistake. A man should own nothing. I have thought about it and am sure of it.'

'Let a man commit no fault, and then what you say will be true. I made a mistake, and allowed myself to be so governed by it as to commit a great injustice. I am aware of it, and I trust I may never repeat it. Such a mistake as that I think that I shall never commit again. But I did it, and I ask you to forgive me.' In answer to this she could only embrace him and hang upon him, and implore him in silence to spare her. 'So it has been, and I ask your pardon.'

'No, George, no; no.'

'Will you not pardon me when I ask you?'

'I cannot bring myself to say such a word. You know that it is all right between us. I cannot speak the word which you shall never be made to hear. I am the happiest woman now in all England, and you must not force me to say that which shall in any way lessen my glory.'